THE GREAT MILLENNIUM MOUNT EVEREST CAT EXPEDITION
& OTHER CAT STORIES

The Great Millennium Mount Everest Cat Expedition & Other Cat Stories

by

Bill MacDonald, author of *Tyke & Dusty*

BOREALIS
BOOK PUBLISHERS

Borealis Press
Ottawa, Canada
2000

Canadä

*The Publishers gratefully acknowledge the financial
assistance of the Government of Canada through the
Book Publishing Program (BPIDP)
for our publishing activities.*

Canadian Cataloguing in Publication Data

Macdonald, Bill, 1932-
The Great Millennium Mount Everest Cat Expedition &
other stories

ISBN 0-88887-270-4 (bound) - ISBN 0-88887-272-0 (pbk.)

1. Cats—Fiction. I. Title.

PS8575.D668G74 2000   C813'.54   C00-901449-7
PR9199.3.M2986G74 2000

Cover design by Bull's Eye Design, Ottawa, Canada

Printed and bound in Canada on acid free paper

Contents

Preface

Following the publication of *Tyke & Dusty* in 1997, I received dozens of letters from readers telling me stories of their cats. At craft markets and book signings, people would stop and relate amusing feline adventures. Many of them had to do with the arrival on their doorsteps (usually in winter) of stray cats. You couldn't help but wonder how these furry orphans knew instinctively where to seek food and shelter. Not that there weren't occasional tricky complications, such as jealous pets already in residence, or a spouse who didn't like cats. But nine times out of ten the situation resolved itself in the foundling's favour, even if, in some cases, it required an attitude adjustment on the part of the designated host. What struck me too was that many of these unsolicited testimonials came from cat owners who were willing, even anxious, to provide details of their own personal lives.

Images of the cat figurines introducing some chapters are reproduced with the kind permission of Pauline Pelletier at the Atelier du Vieux Cap Rouge, Cap Rouge, Québec.

Chapter One

Gumshoe, the Cat Who Loved Motorcycles

After Ashley left him, big Al MacAdoo led a lonely existence. What he missed most, besides Ashley and her cooking, was Gumshoe, her white cat with the black ears. Gumshoe's name derived from the mask he appeared to be wearing, and from his four dark feet, and from his tendency to always be sticking his nose into things, like a detective.

Big Al soon found that rattling around in a silent, empty apartment was positively depressing. All he had

1

left, really, was his bed and his Kawasaki 650 motor-cycle. Ashley had taken the boombox, the T.V. and most of the furniture. Which was only fair, he supposed, since she'd paid for things with her credit card. Still, he found it dispiriting to come home from work as night watchman at the lumber yard and find no breakfast ready. One thing Ashley could do better than any woman he'd ever known was cook breakfast: pancakes, bacon, soft boiled eggs—his favourite meal before hitting the sack.

To compensate for taking Gumshoe the cat with her, Ashley had left behind a flowering hibiscus plant, which resided in a clay pot on the living room floor and which she knew Al hated. So this was by no means a generous gesture. Several times, during the two years they'd lived together, Al had threatened to throw the hibiscus out with the trash. He disliked the way it branched in all directions, climbing toward the ceiling, spreading its spindly limbs, as though eager to engulf him. Oddly, whenever he cursed or disparaged it, the hibiscus, seemingly sensitive to his tirades, would, within a matter of hours, bring forth a delicate yellow blossom. These retaliatory flowerings, while pleasing to Ashley, annoyed big Al immensely. Once, he'd actually squirted Lysol into the clay pot, but all the plant did was drop a few brittle leaves. Al's only sympathizer was Gumshoe the cat, who had once got indigestion from munching fallen flowers and needed to be taken to the Vet.

Speaking of which, Big Al used to say jokingly that he loved black-eared Gumshoe almost as much as he loved Ashley. It's possible he even shed a few tears when the two of them split. One thing for certain, he experienced frequent nightmares, in which he saw the poor cat perched on high objects, such as treetops or telephone poles, meowing piteously, afraid to come down. He also missed the warmth of Gumshoe's furry weight on his feet in bed, when, after a lonely night spent guarding the desolate lumber yard, and while Ashley was clerking at the Kivela Bakery on Secord Street, he snored the day away. He'd be the first to admit that back then he had the world by the tail in a downhill pull, and slept happy, knowing that when her shift was over at Kivela Bakery, Ashley would come home and cook his favourite supper—pot roast with parsnips and gravy.

Ashley moved out, you see, because Al liked to spend his weekends and holidays motorcycling with his buddies. They would saddle up at a moment's notice and ride to Duluth or Ignace or Sault Ste. Marie, and Ashley would be left behind with nothing to do. It wasn't that Al disliked her company, but he was irresistibly drawn to the open road, to the roar of his Kawasaki 650, to the camaraderie of bearded, booted, tattooed, black-leather-jacketed young men he'd known since childhood. Even when Ashley begged him to stay home and take her dancing at Mulligan's, or tempted him with pot roast and lemon meringue pie, the call of the open road was too strong and big Al would have to answer it.

A curious thing is that Gumshoe the cat seemed to like Al's motorcycle too. When Al parked it on the sidewalk outside the apartment, Gumshoe would jump onto the saddle and repose there contentedly. He would curl up and take his afternoon siesta, or groom himself, or just sit and watch traffic. On those occasions when neighbourhood dogs stopped and barked at him, he would arch his back and hiss at them from the safety of his perch. For some reason, perhaps because they knew how much noise the Kawasaki could make if it wanted to, and how it could belch hot exhaust in your face if you got too close, the dogs kept their distance.

But I digress. Last June, the day before Ashley's twenty-seventh birthday, when big Al went motor-cycling westward with his pals, she decided she'd had enough. She was quite certain he'd never change and she was tired of playing second fiddle to a Kawasaki 650. And so while he was away she signed a lease on a bachelor apartment across town, hired a moving van, and after tucking Gumshoe under her arm and leaving Al a curt note of explanation, but no address or tele-phone number, she vamoosed. Who could blame her? Who among us wants to be taken for granted?

When Al returned from Winnipeg and found his lodgings vacant and vacated, he went through surprise, anger, disbelief and self-pity. He took a good hard look in the mirror, trying to decide whether he was a fool or a victim. How could Ashley have betrayed him like this? Hadn't he eaten her cooking without complaint, let her cat sleep on his feet, kept the fridge stocked with beer in case she ever got thirsty? Feeling sorry for him-self, he rode off to work at the lumber yard, and when he came home, went to bed hungry.

That day, and for several days thereafter, Al dreamed a terrible dream, in which he'd become a feeble, friendless old man, too stiffened with rheuma-tism to ride his motorcycle, living alone in a shack on the river, laughed at by rude children. When he woke up, he telephoned Kivela Bakery and asked to speak to Ashley, but was told she was away on vacation and had left word that her whereabouts be kept secret.

Big Al's story might end there, I suppose, had he not glanced out his window one afternoon a month or so later and seen an unbelievable sight. Sitting on the saddle of the Kawasaki, looking a bit tattered and undernourished, was Gumshoe! Al could hardly believe his eyes. He ran out in his underwear to make sure it was Gumshoe. And it was. With dirty fur and broken whiskers. With scars on his nose, tar on his tail and his ribs showing. But it was Gumshoe, no doubt about it.

Al picked him up and carried him into the apartment. He gave him a saucer of Scotch broth, his favourite soup, and half a tin of kippers. He made a fuss over him, until finally, faintly, Gumshoe purred. Then the two of them went into the bedroom, and when Al lifted Gumshoe onto the bed, the weary, limping cat turned a few circles, lay down and fell asleep.

Not knowing exactly what to do, but feeling himself on the verge of a major decision, Al telephoned Kivela Bakery on Secord Street and asked to speak to Ashley. "She's not here," the baker's wife told him. "She doesn't work here anymore."

"Well, where is she?" Al demanded.

"We don't know," the woman said, but Al could tell she was lying.

"I have a message for her," he said. "If you're talking to her, please tell her that her cat has come home, and he's here with me, and if she wants him back, she can come and fetch him. If he left her once, though, he's liable to do it again. He'd rather be here with me. I don't think he likes her new place. Or, if she prefers, I could bring the cat to her. Whichever she wants. Will you tell her that?"

The baker's wife didn't say anything for a moment. Then she said, "Yes, I will. She'll be glad to hear her cat's still alive. She thought it must be dead. She thought it had probably got run over or been savaged by dogs. I believe she'd given up hope. I still don't see how it could have walked that far, across two expressways and a hundred busy streets, through Jumbo Gardens and Mariday Park, past County Fair Plaza, with cars and trucks and crazy people on the road. I don't see how it knew where to go."

Big Al chortled. "He's a smart cat, is old Gumshoe. Maybe he navigated by the stars. Maybe he has a built-in compass, like a Canada goose. The thing is, he wanted to come home, where he belongs. So you tell Ashley for me we'd like to see her, if only we knew where she was. Tell her we won't go off and leave her anymore. Tell her we'll sell the damn motorcycle, if that's what she wants."

The baker's wife clucked her tongue. "Well, now," she said. "Well, now. Wouldn't that be something."

To make, as they say, a long story short: Ashley phoned Al ten minutes later, asked him tearfully how Gumshoe was, and if he was serious about selling the motorcycle.

"You're damn right I am," Al said. "If that's what it takes to get you back."

"There's one other thing," Ashley said.

"What's that?"

"A small thing, really."

"What is it? Not the bloody hibiscus, I hope. It died. I forgot to water it."

"No, it's not the hibiscus."

"What, then?"

"I'd like you to take me dancing at Mulligan's on Saturday night."

There was a long pause, a long silence. Al had to

think about this. You could almost hear the wheels turning. For some reason, the image of a pot roast floated across his mind, smothered in parsnips and dark gravy. He could smell it, could all but taste it. When he closed his eyes, he could see a shimmering slab of lemon meringue pie, and when he opened them, there was Gumshoe, looking at him expectantly. He pictured himself coming home from the lumber yard on cold winter mornings and finding Ashley waiting for him. Really, that was the best part. "All right," he said, sighing a mighty sigh, like wind in the treetops. "On Saturday, if you come home, we'll go dancing at Mulligan's."

And that, I'm happy to say, is exactly what they did.

Chapter Two

Samantha, The Siamese

As a child, Marla lived on Neepawa Avenue in Toronto, just off Dundas, a stone's throw from High Park. Her father, Graham, was head of the history department at Lansdowne High School. Her mother, Elsie, was assistant librarian at the University of Toronto library on George Street. Marla's older brother, Stanley, was off in Thunder Bay, studying hotel management at

Confederation College, the only institution of higher learning in the province that would accept him.

For her tenth birthday, Marla was given permission by her parents to acquire something she'd always wanted: a cat. It just so happened that her Aunt Helen, who lived across town on Battenberg Avenue in the Beaches area, close to Greenwood Race Track, owned a Siamese cat named Pansy, and Pansy had just had kittens. So one Saturday afternoon, while her parents were busy at a Library Tea, welcoming the new writer-in-residence, novelist Clifford Wilkins, Marla boarded the Dundas streetcar all by herself and travelled east to her Aunt Helen's house. There she became the proud owner of the only kitten left, a gangly, cross-eyed, chocolate-point female that no one else had wanted, but with whom Marla fell instantly in love. All day she'd been thinking seriously about names, and had pretty well decided on Samantha. The moment she saw the blue-eyed kitten, she knew she'd made the right choice —this was definitely Samantha.

After milk and cookies with Aunt Helen, and in possession of a list of instructions for raising Oriental cats, Marla set off for home on the westbound Dundas trolley with Samantha in a covered basket. Aunt Helen had told her that the main characteristics of Siamese cats are their eagerness to converse, their intelligence, and their ferocity when threatened. During the streetcar ride, Marla was certainly able to confirm the first of these, because as young as she was, Samantha never stopped talking the whole time. From inside her basket, she seemed to be calling out, voicing her opinions on every topic under the sun. Passengers stared at Marla, and at her basket, and either scowled or smiled. She noticed the motorman glancing in his rearview mirror.

One old lady across the aisle rode four stops without once shifting her eyes. "Do you have a Siamese cat in there?" she finally asked, and Marla nodded.

As Samantha grew, her blue eyes uncrossed and she settled into a very acceptable lifestyle with Marla on Neepawa Avenue. Though she was strictly an indoor cat, she spent hours every day on the back of the living room couch, gazing out the window. Other than Marla's bed, it was her favourite spot in the house. Besides her intelligence and verbosity, she demonstrated true devotion to her adoptive family and a fierce territoriality, as exemplified by the way she hissed and wailed any time she saw a dog passing. After such an episode, talking a blue streak, she would run down to the basement and sharpen her claws on her scratching post.

The year Marla started high school, her mother, Elsie, was promoted to chief librarian at the University of Toronto Library on George Street. One of her first tasks in this post was to welcome the new writer-in-residence, the eccentric (yet supposedly distinguished) poet, Adair Broadmead. Mr. Broadmead, as you may recall, had just returned from a similar stint in Halifax, where he'd been under consideration as poet laureate at Dalhousie. During his tenure in the Maritimes, he had published yet another slim volume of unintelligible verse, entitled *East Coast Entropy*, which had won a host of prestigious prizes, including the coveted Governor General's Award. This in spite of the fact that no one could make head or tail of the poems. Some academicians deemed them brilliant, if undecipherable, others simply scatological. According to Marla's father, Graham, a pragmatic and somewhat cynical man when it came to poetry, it was this very uncertainty that swung the vote in Mr. Broadmead's favour.

As Marla's mother was soon to discover, the author of *East Coast Entropy* was no less bizarre than his unsavory poems. For one thing, he smoked suspicious, hand-rolled cigarettes and drank wine during his seminars. By the smell of him and the tangle of foodstuff in his scraggly beard, he seldom if ever bathed. He had apparently never heard of deodorants. He wore the same black suit every day, the same black shirt, the same black shoes and baseball cap. He was known to place his unclean hands on inappropriate parts of his female students, while at the same time disparaging their poetical efforts and telling them to consider careers in prostitution or pornographic films. He often brought his dog to class, a high-strung beige chihuahua named Pepito, whom he carried around in his coat pocket and allowed to sit beside him on the seminar table. Which would have been fine, except that Pepito yapped nervously for no apparent reason and had the disgusting habit of walking up and down the table, dribbling pungent urine on people's notebooks. Some days, all Mr. Broadmead would do by way of instruction was line up copies of his published works, interspersed with his various awards and medals, and sit staring at them in silence, as though entranced. He might smoke several cigarettes, drink half a litre of wine, then dismiss everyone by belching loudly and waving his hands in the air.

One of the chief librarian's duties at the University of Toronto library on George Street was to invite the new writer-in-residence to her home for afternoon tea. She should do this at least once, and preferably on a Saturday. It was not only customary, it was in her job description. She could invite anyone else she felt worthy —authors, poets, patrons of the arts, influential aldermen. Notable guests over the years had included Pierre Berton, Margaret Lawrence, Margaret Atwood, Honest Ed Mervish, Mordecai Richler, Farley Mowatt, James Reaney and Robertson Davies. Notable no-shows had included Tennessee Williams, Norman Mailer, Ian Fleming, W.H. Auden, T.S. Eliot, Evelyn Waugh, John Robarts and Pierre Trudeau.

The day Marla's mother Elsie invited poet Adair Broadmead to afternoon tea at her home on Neepawa Avenue, a stone's throw from High Park, is still talked about in library circles. Dressed all in black, carrying his chihuahua Pepito in his coat pocket, Mr. Broadmead stepped off the Dundas streetcar at three o'clock one Saturday, was welcomed by Elsie and ushered into her living room. There, the other dignitaries were assembled, drinking tea and being served cakes and fancy sandwiches by Marla. It had been assumed that Mr. Broadmead might read a poem or two, but he soon dispelled that idea. He said he had no intention of performing before an audience of unenlightened plutocrats. He declined to take his coat and hat off. He sat by himself on a chair in the furthest corner of the room and glared silently at everyone from under his baseball cap. There was mud on his shoes, dirt on his trousers. Without asking for an ashtray, he lit a cigarette. He refused Marla's offer of a cup of tea, saying he'd brought his own. From the inner depths of his voluminous coat he withdrew a thermos bottle and began drinking directly from it. Nor would he accept Marla's offer of cakes and sandwiches. Instead he pulled a rumpled paper bag out of another pocket and began munching what looked like hardtack, dropping crumbs down the front of his shirt, flicking cigarette ashes on the carpet.

Watching all this, Marla noticed how quiet the room had become. Conversations had died out as people watched the mute, aloof, distinguished poet-in-residence, Adair Broadmead, eat hardtack and blow smoke at the ceiling. Elsie, understandably, was ill at ease. Things were not going well. She was afraid her guests and colleagues would hold her accountable for the obvious failure of this tea party, her first official function as chief librarian. Having heard of Mr. Broadmead's fondness for wine, she was just about to offer him a glass, when, of all things, Marla's Siamese cat, Samantha, made one of her patented grand entrances. She went and sat in the middle of the floor, surveyed the crowd in a regal manner, like a queen condescending to receive her subjects. It was apparent she expected the adulation due a reigning monarch. When this was not immediately forthcoming, she did what she usually did—she emitted a boisterous, strident, questioning meow. In the silent room, where the clink of tea cups had become the loudest noise, this produced some unexpected results. First, Adair Broadmead let out a vituperative string of expletives, the gist of which was that he hated cats in general, Oriental cats in particular. Then he pulled his chihuahua, Pepito, out of his coat pocket and placed him on the floor. Almost immediately, Pepito, trembling like a leaf, black eyes bulging, sprinkled the carpet liberally with urine. Then he began barking. Then he saw Samantha, and before anyone, including his master, could stop him, he bared his miniature fangs and made a skittering rush at her.

Marla said later that from that point on, things happened so fast as to be pretty much a blur. She didn't know if Samantha had ever been accosted by a shrill, yapping dog before. It's possible she didn't even realize that this was a dog, that she was expected to run from it, climb the curtains, take refuge atop the china cabinet. In actual fact, she did none of these things. Instead, she drew herself up to her full height, arched her back, bared her own fangs, and trumpeting like an elephant launched herself right at the charging chihuahua. This was, after all, her house, her territory, and she was not about to be intimidated. More than that, she was prepared to defend herself, her property, and those entrusted to her care. In other words, she took the offensive.

To Marla, the cat's battle cry sounded like "Tora! Tora! Tora!" It was, she said, as though Samantha were releasing in a single rush all the pent-up emotion that had so frequently prompted her to run downstairs from her observation post and sharpen her claws. Perhaps this was what she'd been waiting for. A split second before contact, she might have been shouting, "Finally! Finally! Let's get it on!"

And get it on, they did.

Those who were there that day said they'd never seen anything quite like it. Samantha gave Pepito two quick slashes across the nose, followed by two more as he came to an abrupt stop. Then she hissed in his face, making the eyes bulge out even further. Then she yowled a bloodcurdling yowl, which may not have been entirely necessary, because by then Pepito was in full retreat, scampering as fast as he could toward his master, with Samantha hot on his heels, still yowling.

Mr. Broadmead, the distinguished, if unkempt poet, stood up then, seized his violently trembling dog and stuffed him into the safety of his coat pocket. To say he was angry would be an understatement. He was livid. He was, as they say, beside himself. His once steely composure had been shattered. He was no longer aloof. Heading for the door, completely forgetting his thermos bottle, he uttered terrible, unpoetic blasphemies. He condemned not only Marla's mother, in her capacity as chief librarian at the University of Toronto library on George Street, but all those assembled, including Marla and her Siamese cat, the ungentle, inhospitable, shrieking Samantha.

Marla says there was awkward silence after that, which lasted until her mother decided to brew more tea and pass around a plate of macaroons. Then, as conversation resumed and giggles eased the tension, people could be heard saying what a boor Mr. Broadmead was, to have brought his dog to a tea party, to have sat in a corner with his hat and coat on, smoking cigarettes and drinking tea from his own thermos. Eccentric poet and winner of awards he might be, but there was a fine line between eccentricity and boorish behaviour. To top it all off, hadn't he called them a bunch of materialistic plutocrats? Meanwhile, as you might have guessed, Samantha was down in the basement sharpening her claws.

But that is not quite the end of the story. The following Monday, Adair Broadmead, award-winning poet and writer-in-residence, tendered his resignation to the chancellor of the library, Mr. Abercrombie. He said he could no longer function amid such a collection of bigots and materialistic plutocrats and had decided to head west to Vancouver, where poets were appreciated and people civilized.

Marla's mother, upon hearing this, and assuming

she'd be asked to step down as chief librarian (because, after all, Mr. Broadmead's departure was her fault), spent the rest of the week preparing her own letter of resignation.

Imagine her surprise, therefore, when, on Friday afternoon, chancellor Abercrombie summoned her to his office and congratulated her for having engineered the timely departure of the most trying, difficult, and unsuitable writer-in-residence the library had ever employed. "We were at our wits' end," he said, "wondering how to get rid of him. Especially as he came so highly recommended from the halls of Academe. It goes to show, you *can* sometimes judge a book by its cover. In any case, we owe you a debt of gratitude, Elsie. I'm not sure how you pulled it off, but you did, and we're obliged. I can see now, if I couldn't before, that you'll make a splendid chief librarian. Anyone else would have knuckled under and allowed this barbarian to subvert the minds and talents of our students. I believe I'll recommend you for a raise in pay."

Elsie could have left it there. She could have said nothing and basked in all the glory. But she didn't. She said, "Chancellor Abercrombie, I must tell you, I can't take all the credit."

Mr. Abercrombie raised his eyebrows. "Oh?" he said. "And why is that?"

"Because it was mostly Samantha's doing. Had it not been for her, Adair Broadmead might still be with us."

Mr. Abercrombie nodded, stroked his chin, looked thoughtful. "I see. And who is this Samantha you speak of?"

"She's my daughter's chocolate-point Siamese. At our tea party last Saturday, she put the run on Mr.

Broadmead's chihuahua, Pepito. I must tell you, Mr. Broadmead was not amused."

Which is why, at the next meeting of the Library Board, chancellor Abercrombie proposed that Samantha, the blue-eyed Siamese, be awarded a citation for meritorious service.

Chapter Three

One-Eyed Jack

These days, One-eyed Jack is a gentle, dignified orange cat, even though his name might conjure up an image of a scar-faced, swash-buckling pirate, with a cutlass in his scurvy hand and a black patch over one eye. It's a good thing he's handsome and mild-mannered, because his job is to greet customers at Gladstone Printers on Mirimac Drive. He's a conscientious cat and takes his work seriously, although by turns he can be playful and slothful too.

Jack was not always as debonair as he is now. It's not known where he started life, but when he was just a few weeks old he was found one rainy morning in a BFI dumpster behind Gladstone Printers. The people who found him were Archie and Hannah Weddell, co-owners of the business, who until that day had no special feelings about cats, one way or the other. Their daughter Daniella, long since married and living in Regina, had never wanted a dog or a cat. When she was seven, she expressed mild interest in owning a snake, but when she learned they ate live mice and baby chicks and sometimes bit their owners, she gave up the idea and settled for a pair of roller skates.

The day the Weddells found One-eyed Jack in the BFI dumpster also marked their thirtieth anniversary in the printing trade. To honour the occasion, Archie had put on his good suit, with the idea of taking Hannah to dinner after work. He'd begun his career as an apprentice at Picasso Printing on Red River Road, had advanced to Rubicon Printing on Cumberland Street five years later, and in 1970 opened his own shop on Mirimac Drive. Hannah had been his first secretary, then his wife, and finally his partner.

On the day in question, they'd just emerged from their car and were unlocking the shop door when they heard what sounded like a young child crying. "Must be the wind in the wires," Archie said.

But Hannah didn't think so. "Sounds more like a cat to me," she said.

With the key in the door and rain coming down, Archie was anxious to get inside, especially as he was wearing his Sunday suit. And yet, it did sound like a cat. Which was ironic, because just recently he'd been saying that what the shop needed to keep mice out of the storeroom was a cat. But there were no cats in the neighbourhood that he knew of. Certainly none that could be hired for part-time mouse duty, or that would be out on a nasty morning like this.

But then they heard the sound again, just as they were about to go in. It definitely sounded like a cat. An unhappy cat. There was a tone of distress in its cry, or perhaps fear. Archie and Hannah stood there in the rain, scanning nearby trees and rooftops. The only animal in sight was a solitary crow on a lamp post.

"If I didn't know better," Hannah said, "I'd say it's coming from our dumpster."

Archie didn't see how that was possible. "Why would a cat climb into a dumpster? There's nothing in there to eat."

"Maybe somebody threw it in to get rid of it."

"Don't be absurd. Who in their right mind would do such a thing?"

Then they heard the cry again. It was definitely coming from the dumpster and it definitely sounded like a cry for help. So Archie went into the storeroom to get the stepladder, and remembered he'd taken it home on Friday to clean out eavestroughs. So he got a chair and put it against the dumpster and climbed up for a look. But the chair wasn't quite tall enough, and so he couldn't see over the edge. Meanwhile, the cat, if that's what it was, though still meowing, sounded weaker, less demanding. Archie had visions of a mother cat with kittens, and was not happy at the prospect of becoming the adoptive father of a whole litter.

"Well?" Hannah said from the doorway, out of the rain.

"I'll need something taller than a chair."

"How about some of these boxes of paper, piled

up?"

"They'll get soaked. Besides, I'm not as young as I used to be. I think we should phone the Humane Society. Or the Fire Department."

But Hannah was already moving cardboard cartons of paper toward the door, pushing them in Archie's direction. When she had four she said, "There, that should do it."

So Archie piled the boxes against the side of the dumpster and scrambled up on top of them. With cold rain pelting him in the face he looked over the edge. At first he couldn't see anything but rubbish. Then he noticed something in the middle of the heap, half buried, soaking wet, with its eyes screwed shut and its mouth open. And that's where the cries were coming from.

"You won't believe this," he shouted down at Hannah, "but there's a kitten in here."

"Didn't I tell you? Can you reach it?"

"Not unless I climb in."

"Well?"

"Well, what?"

"Well, what are you waiting for?"

So, having no other choice, that's what Archie did. He was drenched now anyway. His polyester Sunday suit might be wrinkle-free, but it was definitely not waterproof. He pulled himself over the edge of the dumpster, crawled across the soggy mass of wet refuse, and came face to face with a small, bedraggled, orange kitten. Perhaps not realizing it was about to be rescued, the kitten continued to meow, showing the pink inside of its mouth. In spite of himself, Archie felt sorry for it. He wondered how long the poor thing had been there, crying for help. Probably all night, if not longer. And then he was angry. Angry at the senseless cruelty. Whoever had done this should be thrown into a dumpster and left alone all night too, unprotected in the rain, just to see how it felt. At least, he thought to himself, the kitten was still alive. They hadn't drowned it in a gunny sack.

Down below, unable to see him, Hannah said, "What's happening, Archie? Is the kitten all right? Maybe we should get it inside. Why don't you hand it down to me?"

So that's what Archie did. He picked the soggy, clammy, shivering, still-meowing ball of fur up in his hands, wallowed back across the mounds of garbage to the edge of the dumpster, and lowered the kitten down to Hannah. Only as he transferred it into her waiting hands did he realize how sharp the little foundling's claws were. His fingers felt and looked as though they'd been pricked by thorns.

By the time Archie had climbed out of the dumpster and regained terra firma, he was almost as sorry-looking as the rescued kitten. His hair was plastered to his head, his good suit looked like a grease monkey's overalls, his brow was well smudged with grime. He muttered something about being too old for such gymnastics. According to Hannah, he might easily have passed for a denizen of the dismal swamp.

While she took the kitten in out of the rain, he turned his attention to the boxes of paper he'd used for a ladder. Unfortunately, though the middle ones were salvageable, the top and bottom ones were not. As he splashed through puddles toward the door, soaking his best shoes, he found himself calculating the amount of money the abandoned kitten had already cost him.

By then, the first customers of the day were arriving.

Since Hannah was busy drying the kitten off with paper towels and wrapping it in a printer's smock, and since Kirsten, the secretary, was on the phone taking orders, Archie had to man the front desk himself. Knowing he looked like a drowned rat, he suspected people were laughing at him, and was sure of it when someone asked him if he'd been swimming with his clothes on. "No," he said testily, "I've been out in the dumpster rescuing a cat."

That first day, detecting something wrong with the kitten's left eye, Hannah named him One-eyed Jack. For almost an hour she carried him around inside her sweater. When he was finally dry and warm and a little less frightened, she poured half a carton of coffee cream into a saucer and gave it to him on the sales counter. Though his spindly legs were a trifle unsteady, he gamely set to work with his little pink tongue, and as Kirsten, Archie and several customers watched, he proceeded to lap up his breakfast. With cream on his nose and droplets running down his chin, he seemed to enjoy it. When the saucer was empty, Hannah refilled it, and he lapped that up too. Just as he was finishing, the BFI truck roared into the parking lot and after hoisting the dumpster high in the air and noisily engorging its contents, drove off in the rain.

Though Archie would have gone home and changed into dry clothes, Hannah sent him instead to the A & P for cat food and kitty litter. "Why can't Kirsten go?" he asked, sneezing.

"Because it's not her job," Hannah said. "And it's not her cat."

So Archie went shopping, and Hannah found an old wool scarf in the cloakroom and made a bed for Jack in an empty letterhead box. She put the box on her desk where she could keep an eye on it while she worked, and from that moment on, though he may not have realized it, One-eyed Jack assumed the position of office cat and part-time mouser at Gladstone Printers on Mirimac Drive.

That night after work, instead of going out to dinner to celebrate their thirtieth anniversary in the printing trade, Archie and Hannah took Jack home with them, gave him a bath, a hot meal, and the run of the house. In the morning they packed him up and brought him back to work. Which, fortunately, he didn't seem to mind. I say fortunately, because except for two subsequent trips to the Vet, he's been following that simple routine for the past six years. His days are full, but not taxing. In sunny weather he sits on the sales counter till noon, welcoming clients as they come through the door. He stands up, chirps a greeting, allows people to pat him on the head if they so desire. He is neither fawning nor standoffish, but treats everyone alike. If you choose to ignore him, he won't force himself upon you. When old friends come in, especially those bearing treats or catnip toys, he will roll over on his side and permit a belly rub. He may even extend his paws, capture an unwary hand, and, purely as a show of affection, sink his teeth and claws partially into exposed flesh. Though it is not a good idea to try and extricate your fingers until he's through embracing them, Jack will, if you plead with him, eventually let go.

At noon, or shortly thereafter, and earlier on cloudy days, he breaks for a business lunch with Hannah, consisting of a saucer of instant chowder and a bowl of Meow Mix, following which he takes a nap in his scarf-lined box. Though the latter has been replaced and enlarged several times, it is again showing signs of splitting at the seams. Depending on his mood and the noise of the presses, and if he is resting up for the weekend, Jack may doze till quitting time, or, if the spirit moves him, wander into the storeroom and stalk the elusive mouse. Though he has yet to bag said vermin, or even catch a glimpse of it with his one good eye, he strongly suspects its presence, judging by the little black calling cards it leaves. One of these days, Jack says prophetically. One of these days. Just you wait and see.

Chapter Four

The Computer Cat
or: My Career as a Writer

Okay, I'm spoiled rotten. I'll be the first to admit it. So? I have some annoying habits too. I tear around the apartment at night, shredding newspapers and knocking things over. I barf up fur balls on the furniture. I shed hair. I'm a sloppy eater. I have occasional bouts of flatulence, especially after a feed of boiled cabbage, which I adore. Give me boiled cabbage over caviar any day. Raw fish eggs? Yuck.

There are those who wouldn't agree, but I think I'm improving. I used to be worse. I don't climb the drapes or my roommate's cashmere sweaters in the closet anymore, after he threatened to have me declawed. Not that he ever would. I overheard him tell one of his girlfriends that he only said it to scare me. Which he did. Now I just chew the laces off his shoes. There's something about shoelaces I can't resist. I used to be bad for pyjama drawstrings and bathrobe cords, but now with everything polyester, I pretty well confine myself to shoelaces.

You notice, I call him my roommate. I refuse to call him my owner, because he doesn't own me. If anything, I own him. And I refuse to call him my master. Dogs have masters. Cats have servants. But that sounds a bit egotistical (which I'm not), so I call him my roommate. It puts us on an equal footing, which of course is another fallacy.

Yes, I'll admit I'm slightly less than perfect. Show me a cat who isn't. If things don't go my way, I can be downright difficult. At the best of times, I'm disobedient. But I say, if you want obedience, get yourself a lap dog. Or better still, a jellyfish.

At least I don't go around inviting women home for the weekend (like some people I know), ply them with champagne and lobster tails and chocolate truffles, and then chase them around the apartment trying to get their clothes off. I don't know what my roommate sees in that. I really don't. So much energy expended for so little gain. But he can't seem to help himself. Sometimes the women are still here next morning for breakfast, sometimes they're not. All I know is that those who stay never leave me enough space in bed and keep me awake half the night doing gymnastics. I mean, there's a time and a place for everything. The worst of it is, my stupid roommate tends to encourage them. I like a friendly tussle as well as the next person, but really! The things that go on around here. Some nights I've been tempted to call in the vice squad. I've got revenge a few times by sinking my teeth into a young lady's toe just when she least expects it. You'd never believe the effect that can have. It's worth being shouted at and driven from the room by invective and a hail of missiles from the top of my roommate's dresser. I've had to duck everything from alarm clocks to reading glasses. I once had an expensive wristwatch thrown at me. Another time a hair brush. Any number of books and magazines. Once or twice, even a shoe. It's a good thing cats are fast on their feet. On occasion, I've had to take shelter in the bath tub, or behind the living room couch. Need I say, the women whose toes I've nipped seldom came back, despite my roommate's abject pleadings. Often, on their way out, I've heard them utter ultimatums involving me, but so far nothing's been done. It's funny how short a fuse some people have.

I've never seen a psychiatrist, but I'd say that most of my quirks could be traced back to something that happened to me when I was quite young. I was teasing butterflies on the back lawn one day, when this monstrous bulldog came through the fence and chased me up a tree. I almost made a clean getaway, and would have, except that I sprang too soon and landed too far down the trunk, with the result that the damn bulldog bit off the end of my tail. You talk about pain. I let out a yowl they heard all the way to Current River. I remember climbing those branches like a rocket. I didn't

stop till I'd gone as high as I could go. Then I looked
down. If I hadn't been in so much pain, I might have
laughed, because there was the stupid bulldog, pawing
the ground like an idiot, with two inches of my tail
sticking out of his mouth. I tell you, though, it was no
laughing matter. For one thing, I was disfigured for life.
I mean, a cat's tail is his prize possession. Cats set great
store by their tails. And here was I, with half of mine
missing. It would be like a young man going bald, or a
girl losing her virginity. Well, maybe not quite. But it
was traumatic. And it affected me. To say I felt violated
would be an understatement.

I was thankful for two things. One, that I hadn't been
declawed as a kitten. If I had been, that maniacal bulldog would have chewed off more than my tail. And
two, that my roommate came along just then, saw what
had happened, and beaned that bulldog between the
ears with a big rock. I've never been so proud of him.
Then he helped me down and rushed me to the Vet's,
where they bandaged my bleeding stump, gave me
painkillers, and sent me home to convalesce. Everyone
said I was lucky. That as I grew, my disfigurement
would be less and less noticeable. I think they were just
being kind. The truth is, my tail still looks funny. All
through adolescence, at a time when we're self-
conscious anyway, people called me Stumpy, Mad
Manx, Sawed-off. Long after I'd recovered from the
actual fright, the stigma of having only a partial tail
bothered me, left me with an inferiority complex. It
hasn't been easy. I'm afraid of dogs, of going outdoors,
of loud noises. To this day I have nightmares. I also
can't stand to have anyone touch my tail, or even look
at it. I'm like a person with bad teeth who seldom
smiles, or someone with missing fingers who never

shakes hands. So I make no excuses for my behaviour. If I'm weird, I think I have reason to be.

Perhaps I should tell you, my roommate fancies himself an author. He's never had anything published, and likely never will, but that doesn't stop him from spending every waking moment (when he's not off stocking shelves at the Canadian Tire Store in County Fair Plaza) glued to his computer, pecking at the keys like a deranged chicken. Hour after hour, weekends and holidays, long into the night, he hammers away. If he weren't so serious, it would be laughable. Sometimes he gets so engrossed he forgets to feed me and I have to remind him, none too subtly, that my dish is empty. At such times, I get right up in his face and complain.

As to what it is he's writing, I haven't a clue. If I had to guess, I'd say it's something spooky, something otherworldly. I base this on the fact that he believes in ghosts and spiritualism. He fancies himself a medium, a channeler, if you please. He subscribes to *Mystic Magazine* and *The Automatist*, reads them from cover to cover. He talks to psychics on the Internet, uses words like "telekinesis" and "astral bodies" in everyday speech. He actually believes you can make contact with the departed. I know he's been to seances around town, and has even held a few right here in this apartment. At first, I thought they were only a means to get women to let their guard down. He'd go into a trance and say that someone in the great beyond wanted to see them in their birthday suit, or check them for tattoos. Sometimes this worked, sometimes it didn't. Either way, you have to give him credit. He's nothing if not inventive.

My problems with all this began when he started leaving his computer switched on at night. Seems he'd heard that what wears out a computer faster than anything is switching it on and off. So I'd wake up at three or four o'clock in the morning, as I usually do, take a turn about the apartment, as I usually do, look out the window, have a drink of water and a bite to eat. But then I'd see this stupid computer screen staring at me in the dark, with its blinking, bird-like cursor flashing provocatively, and I'd wander over to see what my roommate had been writing. Of course it made no sense to me, but I got into the habit of sitting at his desk and tapping a few keys, just to watch the letters flit across the screen. A harmless pastime, you'd think. It kept me amused till I got sleepy again and went back to bed.

The only thing was, next day, seeing all these strange, incomprehensible words added to his writing, old You Know Who thought he was getting messages from the spirit world. I'm not kidding. It took him a while to realize this was happening with some regularity, and when he figured it out, he went bananas. It confirmed all his beliefs in supernaturalism. He now knew, beyond any shadow of a doubt, that alien beings were trying to contact him. They had chosen him for obvious reasons, not the least of which was that he was a *believer*. The only difficulty was, they were using some kind of code, or cipher, which it was his duty to try and break. What drove him crazy was that no sooner would he think he had it figured out than I'd add a few more paragraphs and he'd have to start all over. He could never get ahead of it. Some days, he'd phone in sick to Canadian Tire and stay home to work at decoding. He went to the library for books on cryptography, elucidation, interlinear translation. He spent hours on the Internet looking for information on secret languages. He even sent away for an Army Surplus deciphering machine, developed during World War II and guaranteed to "crack any code known to man or primate." He wrote to NASA for their latest pamphlets on UFO's and extraterrestrial phenomena.

I'm not making this up. If it's unbelievable, that's not my problem. My roommate was totally convinced that coded messages were being sent to him on his computer from another dimension, from the hereafter, from Paradise. It might still be going on except that finally, in desperation, he went out and bought a surveillance camera, which he brought home, mounted on the wall, and pointed at his computer. I believe his intention was to catch on film any poltergeist or ectoplasm that was trying to make contact.

Of course, in my ignorance, I didn't know a surveillance camera from an ashtray. How could I? I thought the thing was just another of my roommate's ridiculous wall ornaments. And so it came as quite a surprise to me one day when, upon scanning the tape from the previous night (a night on which I'd been particularly restless and had spent longer than usual on computer pranks) my roommate let out a bellow of discovery, much like Columbus must have done when he found America, or Einstein when he hit upon his theory of relativity, or Newton, the day he got bonked on the head by an apple, or Archimedes, sitting in the bathtub, shouting "Eureka!"

When I should have been seeking a safe place to hide, I made the mistake of running out to see what marvelous thing my roommate had unearthed. It reminded me of the time a few months ago when he found his favourite socks in the towel drawer.

I think what upset him was that he'd spent a lot of time and money trying to solve a problem that had such an easy, mundane explanation. He was also bitterly disappointed that it had been his bobtailed cat, and not an alien life form, leaving messages on the computer.

His pursuit of me on this occasion was fast and furious. We tore around the apartment like Wily Coyote and the Roadrunner. I'd never heard such expletives, not even when I bit girls on the toe and spoiled their ecstasy. When finally my roommate ran out of gas and collapsed on the couch, red-faced and panting, the apartment looked like a war zone. You might have thought a tornado had just blown through. As for me, I found a place in the depths of the broom closet, behind the umbrellas and galoshes, and that's where I spent the morning.

So now, what can I tell you? My roommate has gone back to shutting off his computer at night, thus depriving me of my little game, but at the same time effectively putting a stop to the coded messages from other worlds. The surveillance camera has been removed and sold to the landlord of our building. I have no idea what he plans to do with it. My roommate is back working on his great Canadian novel in his spare time and stocking shelves at the Canadian Tire Store in Country Fair Plaza for a living. He's managed to entice a few girls into spending the weekend with him. Some of them even bring me treats. More like bribes, I'd say, to keep me off the bed at night.

But really, as I said a moment ago, I'm getting better. It's not so much that I'm learning from my mistakes, it's that I'm getting too old and too fat to run and hide every time I commit a misdemeanour. You don't have to bite off my tail or throw alarm clocks at me to get my attention anymore. You want proof? Well, it's been ages since I sank my teeth into a girl's toe in the middle of the night. I'd say that's a good sign. Now, I just go out to the living room and crash on the couch. Sometimes, though, I lie awake wondering how close my roommate came to cracking the code. I mean, I wonder what I said? Wouldn't it be funny if I turned out to be the literary genius? It's not that farfetched. On TV the other night they showed a cat painting pictures with her paws. It looked like art to me.

Chapter Five

Velvet

To look at her now, you'd never guess that Velvet, the Thornton's rusty Persian, was once at death's door. Admittedly, she has a bit of a limp and a crooked neck. Her left cheek is flat, her left eye partially closed. She's missing a few teeth and half an ear. And when she hurries, which isn't often, she tends to stumble. Still, she seems happy. She enjoys simple pleasures and purrs at the drop of a hat. She'll purr when you comb her. She'll purr when she's sitting by herself in the sun.

She'll purr when you make a fuss over her and tell her she's gorgeous. She'll purr and rub your leg when you open the fridge door or use the can opener. She'll purr when she follows you into the bathroom and sits looking at you while you sit looking at her. It's not that she disrespects your privacy, it's just that since you're sitting there doing nothing anyway, you might as well be talking talk to her.

Velvet is nine years old now, but almost didn't make it past two. She was hit by a car at the end of her driveway one day, after being pursued by a marauding dog. The nearest tree was a mountain maple across the street, which is likely where she was headed, full tilt, but she forgot to look both ways. People who saw it happen say she made a prodigious leap (the last leap she would ever make, as it turned out), but caught a glancing blow from the car's front fender. She flew through the air about twenty feet and landed on the grass. Luckily, no wheels ran over her. The dog, a wire-haired terrier, ran smack into the side of the car and thumped his head, but was able to stagger off under his own steam.

Poor little Velvet wasn't so lucky. She lay where she landed, out cold, not moving a muscle. The lady driving the car sat behind the wheel in a state of shock, then climbed out and stood in the middle of the road, wondering what to do. People who had heard the squeal of tires rushed from their houses, afraid a child had been hit. Someone shut off the car's engine. Someone else got the lady to sit down on the curb before she fainted. Just then a Sears delivery truck came along, but couldn't get by, so the driver walked over to see if there was anything he could do. He ended up moving the car out of the way.

It was at that point that Edie Thornton, who owned Velvet, went out to see what had happened. She wasn't worried about her daughter, Courtney, who was at school, or about her new baby, Russell, who was asleep in his crib, but she could see people in the street and wondered what they were doing. At first, she thought the car had hit the Sears truck. But then her next-door neighbour, Mrs. Wrenchuk, accompanied by her sister, Luba, who was visiting from Hamilton, came up the driveway with a very sad look on her face and told Edie that Velvet had been struck by the car and was probably dead. She sent Luba in to baby-sit Russell, then took Edie by the hand and led her across the street. Sure enough, there was Velvet, motionless, bent and bleeding, with people kneeling around her. "The poor thing didn't stand a chance," they were saying.

So Edie started to cry, and Mrs. Wrenchuk tried to comfort her as best she could, and others were telling the lady sitting on the curb that the accident had been unavoidable and she shouldn't blame herself. "Just be thankful," they said, "that it wasn't a youngster."

It was the Sears truck driver who pointed out that the cat's eyes were opening and closing and that it seemed to be trying to move its hind legs. In a strange way, the spectators felt worse about this than if the cat had been killed outright, because now they sensed its agony and didn't want to see it suffer.

And that's when Mrs. Wrenchuk, an ex-nurse, bless her heart, sprang into action. She took off her sweater, wrapped Velvet in it, and carried her across the street. She put Edie in the front seat of her minivan, gave her Velvet to hold on her lap, and drove like fury to the Highview Animal Clinic on Red River Road.

There, the young doctor on duty looked doubtful.

Besides Velvet's visible wounds and broken bones, he suspected internal injuries. Nevertheless, he examined her carefully, felt her all over, listened to her heart and lungs. "Maybe," he said. "But no guarantees. She's suffered major trauma. She'll need some serious surgery. There's a chance she won't make it."

"Will you at least try?" Mrs. Wrenchuk asked him.

"That's up to you."

"It's not my cat. It belongs to my friend here, Mrs. Thornton."

"Then it's up to her. She'll have to make the decision. I'd say the odds are fifty-fifty. The cat's awake and breathing, and has a fair heartbeat. If we're going to try, though, we'll have to start immediately."

Edie, still crying, said she wondered if she should telephone her husband at work. She wasn't sure what he'd say about the cost. He'd never been keen on having a cat in the first place. As a matter of fact, he'd been firmly against the idea. It was only at their daughter Courtney's insistence that he'd finally given in. Lately, after the birth of the new baby, he'd been looking for ways to cut expenses. But then she thought of Courtney coming home from school, of having to tell her that Velvet had been put to sleep.

The Vet said, "Well, ma'am, what's your decision?"

"I'd like you to try," Edie said. "If you think you can save her. If you think she'll ever walk again, I'd like you to try. For my daughter's sake. It's really her cat. She's the one who named it."

And so the Vet summoned his nurse, told her to prepare the anaesthetic and an IV, and carried Velvet into the operating room. "We'll do our best," he said. "She looks like a strong little tyke, and she obviously hasn't given up. It would be a shame to lose her. We'll call you later in the day."

Which they did, fifteen minutes before Courtney came home from school. They said that Velvet was just out of the anaesthetic and had come through with flying colours, considering the damage she'd suffered. They'd patched her up as best they could, put a splint on her left hind leg, removed several loose teeth, sewn up her cuts. Though she'd never be quite like new, and would walk with a definite limp, they had high hopes for her. The thing that worried them was the condition of her back, which, though not broken, had been severely sprained. As well, there was the side of her face, which had been crushed. They were afraid her breathing and eyesight might be affected. But she'd had a big dose of antibiotics against infection, and now all anyone could do was let Nature take its course and see how she healed. "I'll say one thing for her," the Vet added. "If the will to live means anything, she should come along just fine. I've never seen an animal with such fire in her eyes, despite the shape she was in. It's like she was ready to do battle."

And yes, she could have visitors, but that did not mean she'd be going home anytime soon. The thing that had to be guarded against, of course, was pathogenic infection. And visitors must not be upset at finding her sedated, must not expect her to jump up and welcome them. Sometimes, he said, seeing their pets hospitalized distressed young children, so it would be wise to prepare Courtney ahead of time.

As it turned out, Courtney was fine. She not only understood that Velvet was lucky to be alive, she had complete faith in the Vet's ability. Though the sight of her cat's sutures and bandaged leg and bald spots caused her momentary apprehension, she recovered quickly. She gently stroked Velvet's head, talked to her, assured her she was on the mend. And believe it or not, though Velvet was immobile and had tubes sticking out of her, and though there was still dried blood on her fur and both eyes were swollen shut, she responded with the faintest of purrs. And that, according to the Vet, was a very good sign indeed.

But if Courtney handled things stoically, her father did not. Though at first he'd been less than pleased at the thought of spending all that money on medical repairs to a mere cat, when he saw Velvet at Highview Animal Clinic, his mood changed perceptibly. It wasn't that he'd suddenly grown fond of felines, but seeing this rust-coloured creature so battered and helpless, through no fault of its own, seemed to affect him. Later, he would say he'd been struck by the horrifying thought that it could just as easily have been Courtney lying there, instead of her cat, about whom she cared so much. He said he suddenly realized how close a bond his daughter had with this living, breathing animal, who had meant no harm to anyone and yet had been victimized. Before he knew what was happening to him, he was shedding tears and holding Courtney in his arms. He would say later he'd have been fine if the damn cat hadn't started purring. With tubes coming out of it and covered in stitches, it lay there purring, for no other reason than that his daughter was talking to it and stroking its head. How the hell, he wanted to know, could anyone not be moved to tears by that?

When they got home, Courtney reported to her mother and baby brother that Velvet was recovering as well as could be expected and would be back with them in a few days. She said the Vet was very nice, and her father had been very brave, though not quite as brave as she. It was, if truth be told, the first time she'd ever seen her father cry. Knowing he'd been against owning a cat, she hadn't quite understood this, or why he'd hugged her so hard, but thought it best to leave these questions unanswered.

Chapter Six

Paladin, Inner City Cat

I called him Paladin, after the chivalrous knights in Charlemagne's court, because I didn't know what else to call him. I never did learn his name. He may not have had one. He was the colour of cold ashes, with a white chin and one white forepaw. He had pale circles around his turquoise eyes that made him look as though he were wearing glasses. For a medium-sized cat he had unusually large ears, which were silvery on the inside and constantly in motion. He was an alert cat, yet not skittish. His pace was slow and measured, except when he followed the pert young female letter carrier down the sidewalk. I'd heard oldtimers refer to her as the Postmistress, and Paladin had to hurry to keep up, because she walked quickly.

Paladin's home turf was Moss Park in downtown Toronto, just north of Queen Street, halfway between Yonge and Jarvis. I'm not sure what he lived on. Though the park abounded in pigeons and black squirrels, I never saw him catch one. I did see him jumping in and out of garbage cans, ripping open plastic bags, pulling apart half-eaten sandwiches and chewing the meat off chicken bones. I also saw him chase other cats out of the little park, sending them skittering across the street or into dense shrubbery. I suspect that at night he patrolled the back alleys. He bore no visible scars, so I assumed he either avoided serious skirmishes or else won them through conciliation rather than physical confrontation. His sole deformity, if you could call it that, was a crooked tail, which looked as though he'd caught it in a door sometime, or had it run over, or been bitten by a dog.

Speaking of dogs, I never saw Paladin victimized by one. It was as though he owned Moss Park, and everyone knew it. True, most dogs going by were on leashes, but even those that weren't tended to give him a wide berth. Only two or three times during that whole summer did I see a dog make a run at him, and all Paladin ever did was climb the nearest elm tree and wait till the danger had passed. I had the feeling, though, that if cornered, he'd counterattack.

I was teaching an eight-week course at Jarvis Collegiate that summer, and subletting a 15th-floor hovel in the Valley View Apartments on Yonge Street. The room had no air-conditioning, sporadic hot water, and a resident populace of cockroaches. Most nights it was too hot to sleep, which didn't really matter, because with the window open, the street music, the cursing and shouting, the wailing sirens and traffic noises would have kept me awake anyway. Every morning I squirted Visine into my inflamed eyes, gargled with Scope, and put on my least clammy shirt. Then I went down and bought coffee and a bagel at Tim Horton's on Sherbourne Street. Most mornings, if it wasn't raining, I carried my breakfast over to Moss Park and sat on a bench. At that time of day it was usually nice and cool, and the only people there would be the groaning castaways who had spent the night.

Quite often, while I was drinking my coffee and putting together some sort of lesson plan, Paladin would show up. I never noticed which direction he came from —he just materialized. In that respect, he reminded me of a stray cat my Aunt Ida had once tamed. She put food out for it over a period of months, but never saw it eating, even though, every morning, the dish would be empty. She could not for the life of her understand why the cat was so secretive. And then one day, for no apparent reason, it sat in plain view and polished off half a tin of kippers in tomato sauce. Not long after that, it moved in with her.

As for Paladin, he would sit in a patch of morning sun, eyes shut, looking sleepy and disgruntled. I couldn't tell whether he was in the process of waking up or on his way home after a hard night. He would scratch himself lethargically, stretch his back legs, cast an evil eye at the nattering squirrels. On occasion I saw him go and sniff the head or shoe or hand of a snoring derelict, then shake his paw in disgust.

One morning at the end of July, after a night of incessant sirens, I arrived to find the park cordoned off by yellow police tape. There were two cruisers parked on Queen Street and several officers meandering among the flowerbeds, examining the ground. What caught my eye, though, and struck me as funny, was that Paladin was right in there with them, following them around, stopping when they stopped, helping search for clues. As I couldn't get to my regular bench because of the tape, I ate my breakfast standing up. An elderly, sun bonneted lady with a decrepit Welsh corgi on a string came up to me and asked if I didn't think it was terrible.

"I just got here," I said. "What's terrible?"

"Another stabbing. The fourth or fifth this summer already, and it's not even August. Our parks are no longer safe. I don't know what the world's coming to. That's the fourth or fifth dead person I've seen taken out of here this summer. Maybe the sixth. They might as well leave the hearse right here, so they won't have to keep sending for it. And look at those policemen. Do they know what they're doing? I doubt it."

"Did you see the body?"

"No, I didn't, thank God, nor would I wish to. When I got here, they were loading it into the ambulance. It's enough to make you sick. Probably some degenerate wino."

"Well," I said, "maybe that inquisitive cat knows something."

"Cat?" the woman said, jerking her dog's leash when she saw him getting ready to squat on the sidewalk. "What cat?"

"That one over there. He looks like he's trying to help with the investigation."

"If you ask me, there's too many cats. Too many winos and too many cats. This world would be a damn sight better place without them."

So saying, she stamped off down the street, dragging her reluctant dog behind her.

Next morning, the yellow police tape was down and life returned to normal. I sat on my usual bench for breakfast, threw bagel crumbs to the squirrels and pigeons. While I was reading the *Toronto Star* (no mention whatsoever of yesterday's stabbing), Paladin strolled by. "Hello, cat," I said. "Witnessed any good murders lately?"

Surprisingly, he stopped, gave me a thoughtful look, as though acknowledging the fact that he'd seen me there before. I tossed him the last morsel of my bagel, which he sniffed disdainfully before walking away.

In August, my afternoon class started at two o'clock instead of one, and so I got into the habit of having my lunch in Moss Park. It was nice to leave the school and sit under a leafy elm tree. You could enjoy what little breeze there was and relax to the sounds of squirrels chattering and pigeons cooing. The only disadvantage was that by noon the first panhandlers would be stumbling about, pestering you for spare change. If you closed your eyes and tried to catch forty winks, chances are that when you woke up there would be some greasy, smelly, long-haired person sitting beside you, fingers inching toward your pockets.

Across the street from my bench there was a video arcade. It opened its doors at eleven, and within minutes would be swarming with teenagers. You could hear them shouting at each other over the loud music, swearing and bellowing like drunken soldiers. What amazed me, though, was that almost every day I'd see Paladin enter the place, tail aloft, seemingly unfazed by the smoke and deafening racket. Maybe they were his kind of people. Maybe they gave him his midday meal.

Something else that puzzled me was the way Paladin always accompanied the Postmistress to the end of the block. As soon as he saw her coming, in her short pants and straw hat, he would fall in behind her, stepping smartly, like a child following a parade. He would wait in front of each house while she stuffed letters into the mailbox, then hurry along at her heels to the next stop. The thing was, he never crossed Jarvis Street. At the intersection he would raise his tail like a banner, accept a farewell pat on the head from the Postmistress, and then walk slowly back to the video arcade. Even on rainy days he kept to this routine, apparently looking upon it as his duty.

One mid-August evening, when the heat in my apartment was overwhelming, I bought a sausage pizza at Salso's Pizzeria on Queen Street and took it over to Moss Park. Since my usual bench was occupied by two barechested youths smoking joints and drinking beer, I sat on the grass with my back against an elm tree. Not expecting to see Paladin there at that time of day, I was surprised when he put in a brief appearance. He looked surprised too, and was positively astonished when I began peeling the sausage off my pizza and throwing it to him. For once, he didn't disdain my offerings and depart. Sausage was, evidently, more to his liking than

breakfast bagels. He ate every piece I tossed his way, and would have eaten more, except that I eventually ran out.

"Hey, mister," one of the pot-smoking youths said. "Is that your cat?"

"No," I said, "I don't know whose cat it is. I guess it lives around here."

"Yeah, I guess so. But if you don't want that pizza, me and my friend here'll take it."

"Well," I said, "Paladin has eaten all the topping off it, but you're welcome to what's left."

"Paladin?" the youth said. "Who the hell is Paladin?"

The last time I saw him was the day I left Toronto to come home. I was drinking my morning coffee and eating my bagel on my bench in Moss Park when a blue van drove up and parked in the street. I watched as the driver squirmed out from behind the steering wheel and crawled into the back of the van. Moments later a side door opened, a hydraulic ramp was lowered, and down came a middle-aged man in a wheelchair. He had a red beard and shoulder-length red hair and was wearing a sleeveless blue shirt. The size of his biceps impressed me, as did the ease with which he manoeuvred himself off the ramp and over the curb. He wheeled himself into the shade of an elm tree and swung around to face me. On his lap he had a shopping bag, out of which he extracted a newspaper, a peaked cap and a litre bottle of Coke. "Mornin' sport," he said, nodding in my direction. "Be a fine day if it don't rain. Come here often?"

"Every chance I get," I said.

"Seems like a good place to pass the time. Nice and quiet. Nice big trees. Pigeons. Squirrels. Away from the hustle and bustle of Yonge Street. No panhandlers. No dope pushers. Not that they bother me much. Name's Winfield, by the way."

"Are you by any chance a cop?"

"Would it trouble you if I was?"

"Not in the least."

Just then, Paladin emerged from a flower bed and came walking by. His crooked tail was aloft and for a change he looked well rested. He stopped in front of the wheelchair, stood appraising the red-bearded man in the blue shirt. A black squirrel hopped by, but Paladin didn't even turn his head. A whole flock of pigeons landed on the grass, obviously with their hopes up.

"I should have brought some breadcrumbs," Winfield said. "Never thought of it. I'll bring some tomorrow. Will you be here tomorrow, sport?"

"No," I said. "This is my last day in Toronto. But in case you're interested, the cat's name is Paladin and he likes sausage on his pizza."

Chapter Seven

The Augustinian Cats of Bavaria

L ast October we took the train from Munich to the alpine village of Berchtesgaden, on the Austrian border. Besides the famous Bavarian salt mines and the spectacular scenery of the Watzmann Mountains, we wanted to have a look at the 15th century Augustinian monastery, known since the Middle Ages for its carvings of cats. Why the monks back then were so obsessed with cats is difficult to say, but they were. Everywhere you go in Berchtesgaden, you can see the legacy of their handiwork. There are cat carvings and figurines for sale in all the shops—wooden cats, pewter cats, ceramic cats, glass cats, plaster cats, porcelain cats —in every colour and size imaginable. In the monastery itself there is a cat museum, which is full of cat carvings and cat drawings. One of the ancient curators we spoke to said that twice as many people come to Berchtesgaden to see the cats as come to see the salt mines and mountain vistas. Not just German hikers, but visitors from all over the world. Exactly how he knew this, he didn't say, but he seemed convinced it was true.

We took a room with balcony at the Hotel Krone. Checking in, the first thing we noticed was a large, dark carving of a reclining cat on a shelf behind the reception desk. On the other side of the foyer, at the entrance to the dining room, there was another, even larger one. Cathy commented that they looked so real she half expected to hear them meow. The desk clerk, Frau Winzer, told us that both carvings dated from the 17th century and had been done at the monastery. They had belonged to the grandparents of her employer, Herr Grafe, who owned the hotel and had inherited the carvings from his late father. In our room upstairs, she said, we would find similar, though smaller carvings, while in the hotel garden, should we care to investigate, there lurked three cats sculpted in stone and two in bronze.

"What a shame," Cathy said, "that you don't have real cats in the garden, and in the hotel too, for that matter."

Which made Frau Winzer throw back her head and

laugh. "Oh, but ve do, gnadige Frau" she said. "Ja, ve heff katze."

And they did. Upon our return that afternoon from a paddle on the jade green waters of the nearby Konigssee, we were met at the hotel entrance by an elderly brown cat with saffron eyes. The doorman, Herr Garsten, told us that the cat's name was Mieze, and that her half-brother, Seltsam, was also in the vicinity. Both cats, according to Herr Garsten, in past years had been prodigious mousers, and were directly descended from monastery cats.

Though we didn't see Seltsam until the following day, Mieze proved to be a considerate hostess. She followed us through the lobby and up the carpeted stairs to our room, and when we went out on the balcony to taste the air she came with us. It was very pleasant, with a cool autumn breeze off the mountain fanning us and stately Lombardy poplars shedding their leaves. Lights were coming on above and below the village, giving the impression of medieval castles lit by torches. From higher elevations, purple shadows and bands of mist began to descend. It was a truly beautiful fall evening, made even more pleasant by the smell of wood smoke and the cat's gentle purring. Though Herr Garsten had said that Mieze was an avid hunter, Cathy and I found this hard to believe. In her prime she might have been, but at the moment she seemed content to sit and enjoy our company and the October dusk.

At supper that night in the lamplit dining room, the waiter, whose name, unless we misunderstood, was Moos, asked us if we'd come to Berchtesgaden because of the cats. We told him we had. In that case, he said, what we should do, if we wished to see even finer cat carvings and meet the descendants of both Mieze and

Seltsam, was spend some time further up the mountain at the alpine resort of Obersalzberg. In case we didn't know, or had forgotten, Obersalzberg was where Adolf Hitler had owned a luxurious house called the Berghof, and his adjutant, Martin Bormann, had erected a barracks for the Gestapo. But that was long ago, and these days Obersalzberg was once again a good place to enjoy Bavarian hospitality and view the scenery. It just so happened that his brother-in-law, whose name was Osterhofen, managed Obersalzberg's finest guest house, the Hotel zum Türken. If we wished, he could book us a nice room there and arrange transportation.

And so that's what we did. On the weekend we said goodbye to Frau Winzer and rode a Mercedes SUV up the winding, precipitous road to the Hotel zum Türken. From its terraces the view was hazy but spectacular. Looking westward, Cathy boasted that she could almost see Innsbruck. We were given an airy room with a southern exposure, and no sooner had we settled on our balcony to enjoy a basket of fresh fruit and a chilled bottle of Nackenheimer, than down below, strolling indolently across the flagstones, appeared two beautiful brown cats. They stopped from time to time to wash their whiskers and survey their kingdom, obviously in charge, obviously used to being obeyed. Hotel guests on their way to the tennis court stopped to pay homage, and as they patted the cats' heads were rewarded with raised tails and condescending glances.

Just as Herr Moos had promised, the Hotel zum Türken was well decorated with cat carvings. On a shelf in our room sat two ceramic cats with grinning faces. They looked as though they'd just enjoyed a canary for lunch or were planning a practical joke. There were cat carvings in the lobby, in the dining room and in the library, and when we finally met the hotel manager, Herr Osterhofen, he assured us that all these works of art had come from the Augustinian monastery at Berchtesgaden. Before the war, he said, there had been many more cat carvings in the zum Türken, but unfortunately, men like Martin Bormann and Herman Goring, frequent visitors, had expropriated the best of them and given them away as gifts.

Speaking of Herr Osterhofen, it was he who arranged for us to tour Hitler's underground bunker and air-raid shelter, as well as the ruins of his sumptuous Berghof. He informed us that three thousand workers had spent most of 1943 building these structures, which today stand empty and abandoned, grim reminders of a sad time in Bavarian history. When we asked him why his hotel was called the zum Türken, he said that its original owner had in fact been a cat-loving Turk. Unfortunately for him, he had expressed anti-Nazi sentiment in 1937, at the worst possible moment, and before he'd had time to recant, was jailed by the Gestapo and dispossessed of his property.

We asked Herr Osterhofen if the brown cats we'd seen from our balcony were really descended from Mieze and Seltsam at the Hotel Krone in Berchtesgaden, and he said they were. His brother-in-law, Herr Moos, had told the absolute truth. The brown cats of Obersalzberg had indeed been brought up the mountain as kittens. He didn't know if they were products of incest, but somehow doubted it. In any case, all these cats, the Berchtesgaden cats, the Obersalzberg cats, and those at the Eagle's Nest on top of the mountain, were all proudly descended from the brown monastery cats so artistically immortalized by Augustinian carvers.

"Do you mean to tell us," Cathy asked, "that there

are still more brown cats further up the mountain?"

Herr Osterhofen nodded. "Ja, on the very summit, at the Kehlstein, or Eagle's Nest, there are more brown cats. Younger than the ones you see here in Obersalzberg. They would be the grandchildren of Mieze and Seltsam. They belong to my niece, Frau Schuster. From May, when the snow melts, till October, when it returns and the road is blocked, she is in charge of the mountain restaurant called the Kehlsteinhaus. You must go up there before you leave Bavaria, to see the cats if nothing else, though the view is awe-inspiring too. I could book you seats on tomorrow's bus and tell my niece to expect you. She would give you a very nice lunch in Eva Braun's tea room."

So that's what we did. Next morning, after a hearty German breakfast of sausage, eggs, sliced headcheese and dumplings, taken in bright sunshine in a dining room full of tourists from Linz, we went out and prepared to board a Daimler diesel bus. Moments later, a quartet of large brown cats sauntered across the patio in a group, saffron eyes slitted against the sun, looking like palace guards. I don't know if the two we'd seen the day before were among them, but all four ignored us, turned their backs on us, pretended they had more important things to do. Even when we approached them with outstretched fingers and complimented them on the sheen of their fur, they showed total disregard. Not until we were seated on the bus did they acknowledge us, and then only to give us disdainful glances over their regal shoulders.

It is seven kilometres from Obersalzberg to Hitler's Eagle's Nest atop Watzmann Mountain. The narrow road is precipitous and winding, cut for the most part through solid granite. Rounding tight curves, we felt suspended in midair, with sheer cliffs dropping away beneath us. By the time we reached the pinnacle, upon which perches the Kehlsteinhaus, many of the passengers were white-knuckled.

During the ride, perhaps to distract us, our driver had kept up a running commentary in German, French and English. He told us that the Kehlstein, or Eagle's Nest, had been conceived and constructed by Hitler's adjutant, Martin Bormann. who had intended it as a fiftieth birthday present for his beloved Fuhrer in 1939. Unfortunately, though the setting was magnificent and the view fantastic, and though one should indeed have felt like an eagle, or like a Greek god looking down from Mount Olympus, Hitler was not very impressed. Unlike Bormann and Goebbels and Goring and Eva Braun, who all enjoyed the lofty isolation, he spent little time there. Perhaps, our driver joked, along with all his other foibles, the leader of the Third Reich had a fear of heights.

After disembarking from the bus, we entered a wide, dimly lit tunnel and made our way on foot to a gigantic elevator that took all fifty of us up a hundred metres inside the mountaintop. As hair-raising as the bus ride had been, those claustrophobic moments in the Kehlstein elevator were even worse. There was nothing to look at but the damp, black walls of the vertical shaft and no sound except the ominous hum of electric motors. At the summit, we stampeded into the sunlight like convicts freed from prison. Some of us went immediately in search of a drink, others stepped out on the windy parapet to look at the spectacular view. As our driver had said, on a clear day you could see all the way to Salzburg in Austria, thirty-five kilometres away.

Anxious to meet cats, Cathy and I found a table indoors, in what had once been the living room of Eva Braun's spacious apartment, and ordered tea and apple strudel. The walls around us were adorned with cat carvings and statuettes, and we had no trouble recognizing them as reproductions of the Augustinian monks' work. At a nearby table I overheard someone say that neither Hitler nor Eva Braun had been fond of cats, preferring dogs, but that since the present-day Kehlsteinhaus was not considered a monument to the Fuhrer anyway, the feline decorations were entirely appropriate.

No sooner had these words been uttered than two half-grown brown kittens came bounding in from outdoors, their fur on end, saffron eyes flashing. As though spooked by ghosts, they darted among the tables and people's feet, then ran to the fireplace, in which smouldered a few pine logs, and there, like high-spirited teenagers, they staged an energetic wrestling match. Seeing them, knowing they must be descended from the brown cats of Berchtesgaden and Obersalzberg, Cathy and I felt that our pilgrimage was now complete. There were no more Augustinian cats at higher elevations, because there were no more higher elevations. Cathy said it was like watching miniature versions of Mieze and Seltsam. We tried to entice them over with offerings of strudel, but though at first they appeared interested, they were soon distracted by something outdoors, and before we could introduce ourselves, they were gone, galloping off on some very important mission.

Though we were unable to exchange pleasantries with them, we did so with Herr Osterhofen's niece, Frau Schuster, who came and sat with us and treated us to a glass of Kummel with our tea. She said her uncle had phoned and told her he was sending up two travellers who had come all the way from Canada to see brown Augustinian cats. She said she owned three, the pair we had just seen, whose names were Ems and Wesser, and a third kitten, named Baden, who was already a fierce hunter and spent all his time chasing ground squirrels about the boulders. She said it was a good thing we'd come when we did, because in another week or two, as soon as the first snow fell, the Kehlsteinhaus would be shuttered and she would descend with her cats to Obersalzberg for the winter. During the cold months, she said, the road was much too dangerous and there were no tourists anyway, not even skiers, who were content with the snowy slopes of Traunstein and Siegsdorf.

Before going back down in the elevator to catch our bus, we bought a cat carving and ventured out on the concrete battlements to enjoy the view. A biting wind had sprung up out of the north and was whistling through the rocks and stunted pine trees. Cathy said she could well imagine how bleak and desolate the Eagle's Nest must be by early November. Far below, we could see the village of Berchtesgaden, looking very small, surrounded by patchwork fields and thread-like rivers meandering off toward the horizon. It would have been nice to see an eagle soaring above the cliffs and chasms, but we didn't. Nor did we see Frau Schuster's third cat, Baden, who must have been busy tracking prey. We stood there a few minutes, overwhelmed by the view, experiencing a curious sense not of supremacy, as guests might have felt during the war, but of detachment, almost of sadness. Cathy said she wondered whether Adolf Hitler and Eva Braun, dog-lovers, had ever stood on this exact same spot. I said I didn't know, but it seemed likely.

A sudden gust of wind made us shiver. It occurred to me that almost all the leaves had fallen now and snow-flurries were imminent. So I took Cathy's hand and we hurried away from there.

Chapter Eight

The Cats of Saskatchewan Pool Six

The question is, what do you do with an abandoned, derelict grain elevator that sits on the waterfront like a crumbling Parthenon, a blot on the landscape, a monument to past prosperity, but of no further commercial or aesthetic use?

The glib answer is: You get rid of it.

The next question is: How?

Recently, several methods have been suggested and rejected by the bureaucrats. According to some, charges of dynamite, placed strategically around the perimeter, would do the job. Down would come the mighty silos of old Saskatchewan Pool 6, telescoping neatly into massive piles of dusty rubble.

(In fact, that has happened a few times already, without benefit of dynamite, when grain dust has detonated spontaneously and blown elevators to smithereens.)

It has also been suggested that the Army be brought in to rid us of this eyesore. Actually, it was the Army who made the suggestion. That is to say, they offered their services. The trouble was, councillors thought they meant to bombard the elevator with cannons or guided missiles from the heights of Hillcrest Park, or drop smart bombs on it, and having seen too many such bombardments televised (Bosnia, Baghdad, Kosovo, Chechnya, Oklahoma City), they expressed doubt.

Early on, it was suggested that a contract be let to some clever entrepreneur, who would dismantle Saskatchewan Pool 6, starting at the top, and cart it away piece by piece. Who cared how long this took, so long as it was done? The only trouble was, the clever entrepreneur, having removed what he wanted and sold it for a profit, turned his back on the project and departed, leaving an even uglier eyesore than the one he'd started with. So much for clever entrepreneurs.

And so the final solution appears to be the expedient one: leave the elevator alone and let it disintegrate. Though this may take two or three hundred years (it was, after all, built to last), at least it won't cost anything.

A few months ago, when the destruction committee went down to examine Saskatchewan Pool 6 for themselves, they made an amazing discovery: the lofty, cavernous elevator had become home to a large number of cats. At first, the investigators thought there were only a few—say twenty or thirty. But as they wandered

through the empty silos with flashlights, and up into the workhouse, and along the shadowy galleries, from which most, but not all the machinery and conveyor belts had been removed by the clever entrepreneur, they revised their estimate of the cat population to fifty or sixty, and finally to several hundred.

The cats were living on various levels, upstairs and down, like tenement dwellers. Just how much interplay there was between enclaves was difficult to tell. They did seem to have some kind of social structure, like prides of African lions, with lithe matriarchs in charge, guarded by muscular warriors and tended by a staff of nursemaids. At least that's how it appeared. There were even a few old male drones, who lay about looking fat. Someone said it was like a collection of fiefdoms, with cats of all ages living in close proximity and going about their business.

Mind you, since electrical power had been shut off and the windows boarded up, and since the only illumination was from hand-held flashlights, the destruction committee confessed it might have come away with erroneous impressions. But they did see cats, and cats' eyes, looking down at them from different vantage points. In their report to City Hall, that's what they said they saw—cats all over the place.

When the report was read at the next council meeting, several aldermen apparently scoffed at it. "How," they wished to know, "could all these cats survive if nobody fed them?"

So it was pointed out that though the elevator hadn't been used in years, there was still enough loose grain left on the floors of the silos—oats, flax, millet, corn, rye, peas and rape seed—to support a flourishing mouse community into the next century. Not only that, there were pigeons, dozens of them, strutting about and cooing, and you could see the cats eyeing them and fairly drooling at the prospect of tender, juicy squab.

From what was revealed in the newspaper and on the radio, one got the impression that there was great controversy among council members over what to do about the cats living in Saskatchewan Pool 6. It was no longer a question of what to do with the elevator, it was a question of what to do with the cats.

Of those who believed the destruction committee's report (not everyone did—some thought it preposterous), the cat fanciers said, "What harm are they doing? They're at least keeping the rodents and pigeons under control." The non-cat fanciers, however, were not prepared to be quite so magnanimous. They hatched more schemes to eliminate the cats than they'd hatched to eliminate the elevator. Some suggested sending in a pack of dogs. Precisely where this pack of dogs was to be obtained, they didn't specify. Others suggested putting up loudspeakers and driving the cats away by playing loud, repulsive music. Discussion then raged as to what exactly constituted loud, repulsive music. Feelings were hurt and toes stepped on when some councillors' favourite music was classified as objectionable. Needless to say, no consensus was reached and that idea was shelved. It was then proposed that the cats be lured out with tins of tuna and taken away in the dogcatcher's truck.

Perhaps the most novel suggestion was put forward by a young alderwoman who played saxophone in an all-girl band and who thought the term "cats" was being used in a figurative sense. In other words, she thought the real squatters at Saskatchewan Pool 6 were pot-smoking hippie musicians. It was her opinion that these lost souls could be rehabilitated. She therefore recommended sending in a team of substance-abuse counsellors.

And so on, and so on.

The last anyone heard, a vote had been taken and a resolution passed awarding a large fee to a Toronto consulting firm, who in turn funnelled a huge grant of local tax money to the Demographics Department at York University, for the purpose of undertaking an exhaustive study of the hierarchy and social stratification of the cat colony presently occupying Saskatchewan Pool 6. As I understand it, York is to have a synopsis ready in two years time, or three, if it takes that long. Eventually, a detailed report will be filed, complete with recommendations. It is thought there may be an MA in this for someone, possibly even a PhD. Time will tell.

According to the newspaper, the only dissenters to the above motion were those officials who still don't believe there are any cats in the elevator. How doubting can you be? I ask. All you have to do was go down there and see for yourself. You don't have to take anybody's word for it.

Chapter Nine

Ripley, The Inscrutable Cat
or: My Life in Retail Sales

My parents left when I was very young and I was raised by maiden aunts. My childhood was what you might call stormy. I was not well adjusted. My adolescence, if anything, was even worse. I ran with a bad crowd. I ignored curfews. On mild nights, I never went home. In time, I'm afraid I forgot where home was. Though I started off having friends, I became a bit of a loner. I roamed the neighbourhood, getting into trouble, being chased by just about every-one. And yet, strange as it may seem, I wouldn't have traded life on the streets for anything. I had complete freedom. Nobody told me what to do or when to do it. I heard other cats being called in at night and felt sorry for them. They didn't know the joy of staying out till dawn, while everyone else was tucked up in bed, of seeing a glorious sunrise over the Sleeping Giant.

For a while, I tried living at the cat colony in the old abandoned Pool 6 elevator. But even there I found too many rules for my liking. And though there were some weaker cats whom I could intimidate, there was one big tough bruiser named Scaramouche, who, for no reason, unless it was because I was better looking than he was and had no trouble getting girls, regularly beat me to a pulp.

Another thing I didn't like about life there was that the place was ruled by matriarchs - duchesses, mothers superior, dowager queens and chatelaines. All shapes, all colours. Giving you orders, telling you what to do, what not to do. Who needs that? I'm not saying I wasn't attracted to some of the younger ones. Espe-cially the angoras. There were a few I could have settled down with, if they hadn't been so domineering, so conformist, so regulation-conscious. I mean, give me a break. I thought cats were supposed to be independent free-thinkers.

Now don't get me wrong. I'm not saying I didn't have my share of rolls in the hay. I did. With some very attractive, obliging women, who told me I was not only virile, but sensitive too. I think that's what caused so much jealousy among my peers. Word got out that I was a Casanova, a real lady's man, and there were some young jocks, like Scaramouche, who just couldn't tolerate the competition. They gave me a really rough time. Picked fights. Insulted me so that I had to defend my honour. Trouble was, if I was a good lover, I was only a mediocre scrapper. I'll be the first to admit it. I lost more battles than I won, and have the scars to prove it.

Had it not been for that, I might have stayed. I mean, the food was good. No shortage of mice, and someone was always dragging home a dead fish for communal consumption. We had some pretty good feasts. And there was a whole field of wild mint nearby, where we used to go and let our hair down. Though some would disagree, I find wild mint every bit as uplifting as catnip. I really get off on that stuff. I mean, I've practically seen visions! The only trouble is, mint gives you the damnedest hangover. A headache like you wouldn't believe, plus blue Johnnies and the rajah shakes.

Anyway, after I finally pulled the plug and left Pool 6, I went uptown and took to the streets again. Like I say, I was my own boss. One thing, though: food was harder to come by. Some nights I really had to scrounge. A few times I went to bed hungry. And another thing—you sometimes had trouble finding a decent place to sleep. Plus, if I may say so, the women were harder, less friendly, more caught up in their own narrow lives. I mean, some of them weren't even civil. None of them ever called my ugly, or turned me down, but there was never much real romance. Just wham, bam, thank you, Sam, see you around, don't call me, I'll call you, if the kittens have blue eyes, I'll be in touch.

As for the tomcats in my district (except for the dainty ones who tiptoed up behind you and made really disgusting suggestions), they were always swaggering around, spraying everything in sight, staking out territory, blowing off steam about how tough they were. Some of them wouldn't give you the time of day. I have no idea what their problem was. I admit I did more than my share of spraying—people's doors, car tires, doghouses (I don't know too many cats who spray doghouses)—but it wasn't my whole life. I'd try to strike up a friendly conversation in the back alley, but instead of comradeship I'd get something like: "By the way, bozo, this is my turf, my garbage can. I catch you around here again, I'll whip yo' ass. You understand what I'm saying?"

To be honest, there were moments when I longed for a sense of community. Nights when I sought shelter from a cold rain in somebody's garage, or climbed up into a car engine that was still warm to the touch (a practice which became increasingly perilous with the advent of remote car starters), I almost regretted having left the elevator. But what the hell, you can't have everything.

What got me into trouble was when I started spraying the front door of a house on Banning Street. Why I chose to spray that particular door, I can't say. Maybe it was because the guy who lived there, a cat-hater from way back, presented a challenge. He was a thrower, not a shouter. We used to call him Deadeye Dick, because of his marksmanship with an old boot or pickle jar. Long after every other cat had given up and gone elsewhere, I still sprayed that door on Banning Street. Old Deadeye must have had acute hearing, or a sixth sense, because as quiet as I tried to be, he'd fling open the door in mid-spray and start throwing things. Some mornings, so help me, his yard looked like a landfill site.

I well remember the day it all came to a crashing end. It was early morning, and there I was, spraying away, when all of a sudden, from out of nowhere, appears this uniformed lady with a net. Before I can get things shut off and make my escape, I'm well and truly tangled. I did some hissing and growling, but it was no use. They had me. The lady in uniform, Miss Hargrove, was pleasant, just doing her job, but what infuriated me was the behaviour of the man whose door I'd been spraying. He came charging out of his house, laughing like a hyena, clapping his hands, jumping up and down, shouting, "I finally did it, you stupid cat! I got you. You won't be spraying my door or anybody else's for a long, long time. Where you're going, they don't have doors, only iron bars. Your spraying days are over!"

The next thing I know, Miss Hargrove is thanking him on behalf of Animal Control and putting me in the back of her truck. This, I fear, is a bad sign. This is not good. I have a feeling I'm about to lose my freedom. I don't know what's in store, but I'm prepared for the worst.

Driving to the Animal Shelter, my life more less flashed before my eyes. I wished I'd stayed at Saskatchewan Pool 6. I wished I'd stayed with my maiden aunts. I wished my parents hadn't abandoned me. But mostly I was filled with anger toward Deadeye, that gloating snitch who turned me in for spraying his door. Talk about your police state.

At Animal Control I was put in a cage and given a bowl of gruel. I'm a little hazy about this, but I think it was nearly a week before anyone came to see me. I got a few mouthfuls of kibble twice a day, dry as dust and tasting like mud, plus all the water I could drink, and I seem to recall being powdered. The only thing that made life bearable was the presence of two tawny kittens in the cage next to mine. Theirs was a sad story with a happy ending. It seems they'd been born to a single, homeless mother, who, not long after their birth, had been stricken by some fatal disease or accident. With the last of her strength, she'd carried the two kittens all the way from a tool shed on Dufferin Street to a house on Summit Avenue. When the children in that house, a boy and a girl, came out to go to school, they found the mother cat dead on their doorstep and the tawny kittens pressed against her, crying. Of course the kids wanted to effect an adoption then and there, but they already had a dog, Bowser, and so the parents phoned Animal Control, who came and got the kittens and gave the mother cat a decent burial.

After hearing this story, I was not surprised when, two days later, the whole family showed up at Animal Control and asked if the tawny kittens had found a home yet. When told they hadn't, the children set up a veritable clamour, which ended only when their parents agreed to let them adopt the kittens. "We've thought it over," they told Miss Hargrove, the lady who imprisoned me, but toward whom my feelings had warmed considerably, "and we've decided that old Bowser will just have to get used to the idea of being a Dutch uncle."

So Miss Hargrove took the tawny kittens out of their cage, gave them their shots, and that's the last I saw of them. But you know, I still can't get them out of my mind. It's not just that they were the first cats I'd heard purring in ages. And it's not just that they had the same shade of fur and markings as I do, and the same colour eyes. It's more than that. There was something about them, something strangely familiar. They reminded me of someone I'd known in the back alleys of Banning Street, someone with whom I'd shared a few cold winter nights. What I'm saying is, I can't help but wonder if I knew their mother. In a Biblical sense.

It's funny how unpredictable fate is. If anyone had told me I'd be taken off the streets in a net and incarcerated by Animal Control, I'd have said phooey. But I was.

Yet life in captivity wasn't all bad. I admit I gave up my freedom (not that I had any choice), but in exchange I got room and board, my nails clipped, beneficial dustings of flea powder. I also got visitors. People came in and looked me over, said how handsome I was, and what nice eyes I had. That's always good for the ego. A not so pleasant comment I sometimes heard was that my temperament wouldn't win any prizes. Seems I had a tendency to spit at those who criticized me and ignore those who didn't. In my defence I would point out that I was, after all, confined to a cage, with no filth to roll in, no pungent odours to get high on, and no women. It's true what they say about prison—the worst thing, after your loss of freedom, is your loss of hanky-panky.

Which brings me to something I don't like to talk about, but feel I must. After I'd been there a while, a very nice older lady stopped in front of my cage one day and said to Miss Hargrove, "I'd like that one, the tawny one with the nice eyes. He's the one my son and daughter-in-law told me about. My grandchildren have two small kittens that look just like him. Actually, it was their idea that I come down here and see this cat.

You see, Miss Hargrove, I'm looking for an attractive animal to grace the window of my pet supply store on Red River Road. Perhaps you've heard of it - Pamela's Pets? I don't want a kitten, because kittens are too rambunctious. I want a calm, mature cat, one with poise and dignity, who will sit still and let people fondle him. I've read that customers enjoy such contact and will spend more. These days, in retail sales, you must strive to stay ahead. My competitor on Court Street employs two cats, a Scottish Fold and an Abyssinian. They're really quite smug about it."

But Miss Hargrove, my jailer, wasn't so sure I'd be suitable for such work. She said she had concerns about my disposition. She wanted to show Pamela a Manx that had just been brought in, and a brown Tortie with mismatched eyes.

"You don't seem to understand, Miss Hargrove," Pamela said. "I want this one. My grandchildren would disown me if I adopted a Manx or a Tortie with mismatched eyes. For reasons which I don't quite grasp, they've insisted that I name my cat Ripley. As for his disposition, surely that will improve once he's been fixed, won't it?"

Which, I must say, got me focussed. I remember standing rigidly to attention. A thousand thoughts raced through my mind. For one thing, I wasn't broken, and therefore didn't need fixing. For another, I wasn't sure I wanted to spend the rest of my life flogging vacuum-sealed punnets in a pet supply store. But then, on the other hand, I'd about had it with living in a cage. And since going back to the streets appeared out of the question, at least for the moment, I was really in no position to be choosy.

The night before my operation, I didn't sleep a wink.

I mean, what can I say? I was petrified. After lights out, I asked if anyone knew what "fixing" entailed. From nearby cages, indeed, from the entire gallery, came muffled laughter. I heard someone say, "Don't ask. You don't want to know. By this time tomorrow, when the anesthetic wears off, you'll have your answer. Just be thankful you're getting out of here alive."

Thus reassured, I spent the rest of the night hunkered in the furthest corner of my cage, dreading the moment when daylight crept through the window and I heard footsteps approaching. That my once carefree, vagabond life had come to this, I found hard to believe.

What do I remember? I remember thinking how gentle the Vet's hands were, yet how firm, as he put me on a table and covered me with a cloth. I remember the nurse's soft, musical voice and the way she stroked my cheek. I remember thinking: no matter what happens, this is the first time in a long time I haven't had to worry about defending myself, about getting beat up, or searching garbage cans for edible food. Nobody was pelting me with pickle jars. I remember the smell of chloroform. I remember a fleeting image of green fields and bright sunshine, and then a warm, peaceful, floating sensation. Whatever they were using was a thousand times better than wild mint.

When I woke up, I felt pretty well. A little groggy, of course, but better than I'd expected. It was dim and quiet in the recovery room. Miss Hargrove, my old friend, brought me a long, cool drink of water. Nothing had ever tasted so good, yet in my lassitude, all I could do to thank her was flick the end of my tail. She seemed to understand, and patted me on the shoulder. "You'll have a different outlook on things now, Ripley," she said.

"And people won't be phoning me to come and arrest you for spraying their front door. I just hope Pamela realizes what a good cat she's getting."

I think Pamela does. I don't much like the name Ripley, but since she paid my bail and treats me like a prince, I can't complain. I sit in the window of her pet supply store on Red River Road and blink my eyes at people going by. I'm amazed at how many of them stop and tap the window, then come in and talk to me. In the old days, I'd most likely have said, "Keep your scuzzy hands off, Dipstick, unless you have a yen for mutilation." But now, such familiarity doesn't bother me in the least. If truth be told, I rather enjoy it. I find it easy to purr, and if I'm in the mood, I'll roll over on my back and expose my belly. This always gets a reaction, and before you know it, the gullible customer is loading up on catnip toys or decorative flea collars or scratching posts or virtual birds or tinned rabbit or some other high-priced delicacy they could buy in a grocery store at a fraction of the cost. But, as Pamela tells us at staff meetings, that's the name of the game.

And yet, I'd be less than honest if I said I didn't sometimes sit and think about the old days. I don't mean that my head is constantly full of lustful thoughts the way it used to be (whatever the Vet did seems to have cured me of that), but I often wonder what's become of the gang from Banning Street, of old Scaramouche, and the commune down at Sask Pool 6. I wonder would they smile if they could see me now? Or would they shudder and shake their heads?

All I know is that my scars have healed and I get three squares a day. Plus snacks. Plus regular hits of quality nip. Plus weekly combings. These days, I can look out my window and see a cute little number go by and not get overheated to the point where I feel I have to pursue her. Which is not to say that the ladies no longer notice me. They do. I haven't lost it yet. Not a day goes by without two or three of them glancing in and giving me that old come-hither look. But now, all I do is act suave and aloof. Sometimes I wink. Sometimes I twitch my whiskers. It drives them crazy, I can tell. Pamela will say, "Is that a friend of yours, Ripley? An old flame? Someone from your past?"

But all I do is shrug.

Cats are, as everyone knows, inscrutable.

Chapter Ten

Cats in High Places

In terms of elevation above sea level, the highest cat I've ever seen was at a remote Customs post in the Andes, on the border between Argentina and Chile, 750 kilometres south of Santiago. Cathy and I were on our way by bus from Bariloche to Puerto Montt. After winding our way up and over the mountains on a precipitous dirt road, bumping along through jungle and rain forest, we descended into a mist-filled gorge, and there, on the rugged hillside, were ordered to disembark with our passports and undergo inspection by Chilean officials.

The building was damp, humid and poorly lit. Our nostrils were assailed by the smells of stale tobacco, perspiration and faulty plumbing. And yet, as with most border guards, these silent, unsmiling men, though wearing ragtag uniforms and greasy caps, and puffing cigarettes as they worked, pretended to take themselves very seriously. They scrutinized our documents with dull eyes, went through our luggage, looking for God knows what. They may simply have been curious to see what we had. Envy may have played a part. It seemed to me they took longer examining the women's suitcases than the men's, running their dirty hands through the underwear, holding items up to the dim, watery light. Momentarily, I had the sensation of being admitted to a penitentiary, rather than to a country supposedly anxious for tourists.

In the midst of all this, as we stood in line waiting to be processed, a large, long-haired, ivory-coloured cat came wandering through. Cathy commented that its fur was the shade of old piano keys. It had large feet, pale green eyes and slightly tufted ears, as though one of its distant forefathers might have been a cougar. The trouble I have with cats, no matter where I meet them, is that I want them to like me. Which is why I always extend a hand and try to make contact. If they'll let me, I pet them, scratch them under the chin and behind the ears. If they prefer a more distant relationship, I can live with that, so long as we do exchange pleasantries.

Of course I've been disappointed many times. Some cats are by nature aloof and do not entirely trust strangers. It may be something in their genes, left over from a time in history when members of the Felidae race were persecuted.

This ivory Chilean cat, however, responded to my advances like a long lost lover. When I clucked my tongue and said, "Puss, Puss, Puss," it ran right to me. Without a moment's hesitation it leapt up onto the long wooden table upon which our luggage lay, and rewarded me by rubbing its cheek lovingly against my outstretched hand. Not content with that, it then stood up, put its forepaws against my chest, and before I had time to guess its intentions, climbed into my arms. Which of course I didn't mind at all. Since I wasn't going anywhere, I stood there holding this large, pale armful, like a woman holding a baby, and was aware of people smiling. It occurred to me that the Customs officers would have done well to take lessons in hospitality from their unpaid mascot, who, by this time, was vigorously buffing the underside of my chin with the top of its head and purring like a gravel crusher. I had never in my life heard a cat purr so loud. Its whole body vibrated. People at both ends of the inspection line turned to see where the noise was coming from.

When it was finally my turn to be examined, I was still holding the cat. Jokingly, I said, "Is this your drug-sniffing cat?" But the agent thumbing through my passport, surly to the point of being rude, neither smiled nor said anything. It may be that he didn't understand English. Never once did we make eye contact. Watching him go through my clothes and toiletries, I felt mildly violated. When he came to my supply of insulin and needles, he held them up as though they were explosives. Still not looking at me, he rattled off a barrage of questions in Spanish.

"Diabetes," I said, and showed him my Medic Alert bracelet.

Not satisfied, he spoke sharply to one of his colleagues, who came over and had a look too. They seemed undecided as to what to do, until suddenly the first officer scooped up all my paraphernalia, set it aside, and shook his head at me. Then he wagged his finger. I was half expecting him to draw his revolver. Instead, he fired off another volley of Spanish, which sounded more like threats than questions. During all this, he never once looked me in the eye. I was aware of an ominous silence, interspersed with the cat's loud purrs and the grumblings of my fellow travellers, who were growing impatient at the delay.

Finally a lady behind me, wearing hiking boots and carrying cameras, binoculars and a backpack, said something to the guard in Spanish. I detected the word "diabetic" several times. At long last, and very reluctantly, the guard threw my needles and bottles of insulin back in my suitcase, slammed it shut disdainfully and shoved my passport into my hand. Visibly irritated, spitting his cigarette out on the floor, he motioned at me to move on. I suppose had he wanted to, he could have turned me back. I would have liked to ask him whether he objected to tourists in general entering his country, or just insulin-dependent ones.

Not until we were back outside in the mist did I realize I was still holding the ivory cat. Now, though it was still purring, it seemed to be asleep. So I disengaged its claws from my sweater and placed it on a bench outside the Customs office, among a group of dirty-faced urchins who were chattering away at us in

Spanish and holding their hands out for money.

As Cathy and I prepared to board the bus that would take us down to Puerto Montt and the Chilean sea coast, I became aware that people were laughing at me. How cruel, I thought, to mock another's misfortune. Then I realized that Cathy was laughing too. "Look at your sweater," she said, pointing.

When I glanced down I saw that the front of my wooly black sweater, which I'd worn in case the trip over the Andes proved chilly, was solidly covered with ivory-coloured cat hair. I looked as though I'd just climbed out of a snowbank, or spilled a carton of milk down my chest.

It took days to pluck off all those hairs, which clung like chinchilla. Not that I worked very hard at removing them. As we travelled down to Punta Arenas on the Strait of Magellan, they reminded me of the friendly cat who had welcomed us so warmly at the border.

*   *   *

Later on that South American tour, we spent two weeks in Buenos Aires. It's a noisy, crowded, vibrant, polluted, fascinating city, with its tango clubs, its ancient church of San Ignacio, its Plaza de Mayo, its towering Obelisco, its bustling Galerias Pacifico, its Museo Nacional de Bellas Artes. But what I found most interesting was its famous graveyard, the Cemeterio de la Recoleta, at the end of Avenida Alvear. This vast burial ground, full of sculpted tombs and concrete mausoleums, was only five minutes from our hotel, and so we spent quite a bit of time there. It's where Eva Peron lies enshrined, and the boxer Luis Firpo, surrounded by the statues and sepulchres of hundreds of their illustrious (and not so illustrious) countrymen.

But what really intrigued me about the Recoleta Cemetery was its huge population of resident cats. We became aware of them the moment we set foot inside the main gate. Besides the cats we could see, peering down at us from the cupolas of the mausoleums, you had the feeling there were many more watching you from the nooks and crannies, from among the cherubs, gargoyles and angels which adorn the rooftops of these vaults. It's a perfect place for cats. Buckminster Fuller couldn't have laid out a better setting. Alongside the walks and avenues there is plenty of grass. There are flower beds and shade trees. You can tell by looking that mice and songbirds abound. Besides, just as in the parks of many big cities, people bring offerings for the cats, bits of meat and fish, table scraps. Who knows why? Maybe they do the same thing for dogs, though I doubt it.

The cats of Recoleta Cemetery in Buenos Aires, at least the ones we encountered, are fairly unapproachable, however. If you get too close to them, they back away, viewing you with distrust. If you leave a tidbit on a grave, or at the base of a headstone, they will sit warily nearby, waiting for you to depart. Unlike monkeys in some parts of the world, who snatch food from your hand and run off with it, the cats of Recoleta keep their distance. Perhaps the competition is less severe. Perhaps their main diet is what they catch on the hoof, not what they scrounge.

Cathy and I lacked the courage to visit this sprawling graveyard at night. I'm not even sure it's open then. But if it is, can you picture all those pairs of eyes glowing in the dark? Can you hear the catcalls, the yowling? It must be a veritable primordial symphony.

One cannot help but wonder how such a society would be structured.

*   *   *

Two blocks from Funchal harbour on the Island of Madeira, a stone's throw from the Hotel Liberdade on Rua Rodrigo, there is an ancient, grass-topped, crumbling stone wall. It is approximately sixty metres long and twelve metres high. Up until 1832 it separated the Funchal Franciscan monastery from the town's waterfront district. On December 31, 1832, fire broke out in a warehouse on the town side of the wall. It burned for three days. When it was finally put out by a deluge of rain, no structures remained standing on Rua Rodrigo. None, that is, except the Franciscan monastery and its stone wall. A year later, the monastery itself was vacated, when the monks moved to more remote quarters at the top of nearby Mount Augusta. They sold their monastery to the Dom Pedro winery, who, to this very day, use it to store their oaken casks in. It also houses a restaurant, a viticulture museum and a large room in which groups of tourists assemble to taste wine

and hopefully purchase a case or two.

Over the years, the cobblestone courtyard on the other side of the wall has been used mainly to accommodate a weekly farmer's market, although sometimes weddings and political demonstrations of one kind or another are held there. Despite storms, wars and earthquakes, the wall itself still stands. Some of its stones have fallen off the southern end, creating a sort of jagged set of stairs to the top. Though too narrow and precipitous for human ascent, sure-footed cats find it perfect. Every so often the city fathers debate declaring the wall a dangerous eyesore and tearing it down, but for various, unclear reasons, they never do. In fact, it has become a sort of historic landmark for the town of Funchal, like the Roman ruins at Ephesus. Tourists enjoy having their photographs taken in front of it. Flowers, especially orchids, that appear nowhere else on the island of Madeira, bloom there in summer. Most people have forgotten who built the wall, or why, or when. Some think it leads a charmed life because it was blessed by the monks back in the early nineteenth century. There is a story in some guide books to the effect that an agile young Moor from Mauritania once climbed it and, because of unrequited love, jumped to his death on the cobblestones below. The guide conducting the tour Cathy and I were on, a girl of about sixteen with braces on her teeth and a ponytail, actually pointed to a dark discoloration on a particular cobblestone and told us it had been stained by the Moor's blood.

Maybe it was. I'm not about to gainsay a sixteen-year-old girl with braces and a ponytail. What I do know is that the day we went to taste wine at the Dom Pedro winery and view this notorious stone wall, there were fifteen cats lined up across its summit. While the guide told us the Moor's story, I counted them. Though they may all have been related, there was a nice variety of shapes, sizes and colours. Some were sleeping, some were bathing, some were simply looking down at us. It seemed to me that the ones looking down wore smug expressions on their faces. They were up there, unruffled, cool as cucumbers, far removed from the turmoil of the streets, unconcerned with the pedestrian problems of commonfolk. Indeed, up there among the grass and rare flowers, they were like monks, with nothing more pressing to do than snooze away the hours and meditate. Or maybe I was reading too much into it. Maybe they were just curious about us. I really don't know. The odd thing was that when I counted again, there were seventeen cats. Having counted carefully both times, I didn't see how this was possible.

*   *   *

It was one of those sights you'd have to see to believe.

We were having afternoon drinks on the terrace of the Château Frontenac in Quebec City. It was a beautiful summer's day, and there we were, perched above the mighty St. Lawrence, watching ships go by far below, soaking up sunshine. Multinational tourists were walking along the Promenade des Gouverneurs, some on their way to the Citadel, others to the nearby Plains of Abraham, where a re-enactment of the battle between Wolfe and Montcalm was scheduled for three o'clock.

Just prior to our fourth gin and tonic, we looked up and saw an elderly man, dressed in white, come riding by on an adult-size tricycle. He wore a white Panama hat, a white shirt, white shorts, white socks and white shoes. His only non-white piece of apparel was a shamrock-green neckerchief. But the most peculiar thing of all was that bouncing along behind him, as sedate as you please, in a little two-wheeled, canopied cart attached to the rear of the tricycle, was a heavy-set, yellow cat. It too was wearing a shamrock-green neckerchief, and looked completely unfazed, glancing left and right to take in the sights, like a potentate on a state visit.

The man in white parked his tricycle at the edge of the esplanade, climbed off, tipped his hat to a gaggle of Japanese tourists as they photographed him. Then he lifted the yellow cat out of its cart and placed it on the grass. The first thing the cat did was stretch its hind legs, then its front, as though having just completed a long journey. Then it lay down and rolled over several times. Meanwhile, the man had taken a picnic basket out of the two-wheeled cart and carried it over to the

edge of the terrace where we were sitting. The yellow cat came strutting along behind him, waving its tail in the air, stopping every now and then to sniff flowers. I wasn't sure if it was a friendly cat, but taking a chance, extended my hand and spoke to it. After only a moment's hesitation, it came over and gave me a quizzical look, as if to say, "Yes, what do you want? I have things to do, so don't waste my time."

I told the man in white he had a beautiful cat and asked its name.

"Il s'appelle Honoré," he said, sitting down on the grass. "Et moi, je suis Monsieur Leblanc."

From the picnic basket he removed paper plates, a bottle of wine and a long-stemmed glass. After uncorking the wine and tasting it, he unwrapped cold chicken, bread, cheese and pâté and began to eat. It was on the tip of my tongue to ask him if he came here often for lunch, to the Promenade des Gouverneurs, under the shadow of the Château Frontenac. But I refrained, because it was quite obvious that he did. He gave Honoré some pâté and chicken too, offering it to him in small morsels on one of the paper plates. Honoré ate a bit, left a bit, and went wandering off through the flowers. A few minutes later I saw him dig a small hole among the pansies and sit on it, gawking about like a regular tourist.

What surprised us, during the hour or so that Monsieur Leblanc and his cat were there, was how many people stopped and talked to them. Some took pictures, but many just said hello and kept walking. Small children would come over and pet Honoré, who seemed to think it his duty to sit beside his owner, looking photogenic, permitting everyone from toddlers to grownups to touch him. Even after Monsieur Leblanc put his

Panama hat over his eyes and stretched out on the grass for a postprandial nap, Honoré continued to sit there, taking the occasional nibble of chicken and pâté, meandering over to the flower bed for a moment of privacy.

The two of them might have stayed longer, but at three-thirty a corps of marine cadets came marching down the esplanade. Though the racket of their passage didn't seem to bother Honoré, it woke Monsieur Leblanc, who sat up and rubbed his eyes, and when he saw where the noise was coming from, straightened his hat and saluted.

We were sorry to see him go. It would have been interesting to talk to him, ask him about himself, learn the life story of his yellow cat. We watched him put the cork back in his wine and repack his picnic basket. Then he lifted Honoré into the canopied cart, straddled his tricycle, and rode off in the direction of Dufferin Terrace. In the distance, down on the Plains of Abraham, we could hear musket fire and the shouts of soldiers locked in mortal combat. Cathy said she would not have been surprised to look down and see a flotilla of British warships sailing up the St. Lawrence past Ile d'Orléans.

Fortunately, our waiter, gifted with intuition, as any good waiter should be, came by just then to see if we needed our drinks replenished.

* * *

My friend Paddy Lipscomb and his wife Dodie have a place in the country on Townline Road. They bought it several years ago as a weekend retreat. Other than a disused pig pen and a collapsed stable, it consists of a few acres of alders and second growth poplar, an old farm house which they gutted and remodelled in rustic style, and a small white barn with green trim. Actually, the barn is in the best shape of any of the buildings. It was the last thing the previous owners painted before moving to town. They'd kept rabbits, cows and goats in it, and had stored hay up in the hayloft.

What the Lipscombs didn't realize, because no one had thought to tell them, was that along with barns come barn cats. The first they knew of this was when they saw one, looking out the hayloft door. "There's a cat up there," Paddy informed his wife, who didn't need to be informed, as she'd already seen it herself. It was a smallish, off-white cat with a black forehead. When Paddy went toward the barn, the cat turned and fled. This led him to surmise that it was not a friendly cat, nor possibly even a tame one. Which was fine, because neither he nor Dodie believed that cats belonged in the house anyway.

They saw the cat quite often after that, usually up in the hayloft, looking out the door, but sometimes running across the yard with a sparrow in its mouth. This sight didn't please them, because they were fonder of birds than they were of cats. It was Paddy's theory that though the barn probably abounded in mice, for a change of diet the cat sometimes went afield. What Paddy found odd was that the cat would take its quarry home to eat, rather than devour it on the spot.

"You have to give it credit," Dodie said. "It's self-sufficient and no doubt a good hunter. To survive on its own, it would have to be. Makes the pampered pets in the cat food commercials look like sissies."

During the summer, they didn't see much of the cat, and wondered if it was feasting on barn swallows, who had nests in the gable ends. Paddy thought it might be, and wondered if he should shoot it, but Dodie said she couldn't imagine a cat climbing through thin air and hanging upside down. An owl or a snake, maybe, but not a four-footed animal. And besides, they did sometimes see the cat, early in the morning, or at dusk, hurrying purposefully home from the alder grove with a feathered trophy. Sometimes Dodie would express grudging admiration. All Paddy ever expressed was anger.

One day in the fall, after the songbirds had all flown south, Dodie caught a fleeting glimpse of a second cat. Paddy had just come home from partridge hunting in the alder grove, chagrined at his lack of success, and found Dodie staring up at the hayloft door. "I believe our cat has a friend," she said. "A moment ago, I saw the two of them sitting up there, looking down at me. The other cat seemed bigger and was quite dark, maybe black or brown. I can't say for certain, but I think it's lame. When I went over and spoke to them, our cat took off for the rafters, but the other one seemed to be dragging its hind end. It took much longer to disappear."

"*Our* cat?" Paddy said, brandishing his shotgun. "It's not our cat. We don't have a cat. Out of the goodness of our hearts we allow it to live in the barn, but it's not ours. I wonder whether I shouldn't put it out of its misery right now?"

But if Dodie wasn't smitten with cats, she was even less smitten with frustrated hunters shooting them for sport. "You'll do nothing of the kind, Patrick Lipscomb!" she said. "That would be cruel and disgusting. It's not bothering us, and I'm surprised you'd even think such a thing. Just because you'd didn't bag a ruffed grouse."

"I don't hunt ruffed grouse," Paddy said grandly, his ego bruised. "I hunt the mighty partridge."

Next day, wondering about this second cat, they took a flashlight and went into the barn to investigate. Though disused, or at least used only for storing hay, it still smelled like a barn, still retained the aroma of the live-stock it had once sheltered. Climbing the rickety ladder to the hayloft, Dodie said that the odours brought back sudden and vivid memories of visiting her uncle's farm at Uxbridge when she was a little girl, of playing hide-and-seek in the fragrant straw with her cousins. She said it seemed like only yesterday, and she could al-most hear their voices.

And then suddenly, from the depths of the loft, they heard a low growl. In the dim light from the door they saw the white cat running away. With the flashlight on it, they watched it retreat, expecting it to disappear. But it didn't. To their surprise, it stopped and turned to face them, obviously afraid, yet standing its ground against their intrusion.

"Maybe it has rabies," Paddy whispered, shining his light in the cat's eyes.

"No, it doesn't have rabies," Dodie said. "It's upset that we invaded its space. How would you like it if some idiot torchbearer came busting in on you?"

It was then they realized that the growling was not coming from the white cat at all, but from what looked like a storage bin full of old gunnysacks. When Paddy shone his flashlight on it, the mystery of the second cat was solved, because there it lay. It was indeed black or brown, just as Dodie had said, and she was right about it being lame too. As they watched, it dragged itself out from under the sacks, covered with bits of straw; but then, finding its escape route blocked, reassessed the situation and crawled back in. Its defiant growl had changed to a plaintive whine of protest, as though it knew it couldn't get away safely, yet resented the bright light in its eyes.

Describing the scene later, Dodie said she noticed feathers scattered about, and knew in an instant where the white cat had been taking all those birds. It had been carrying food to its handicapped friend. Not just easy-to-capture food, but food that required it to leave the safety of the barn and travel quite some distance. When she realized this, she said, she felt such a flood of admiration for the white cat that she almost burst into tears. She said that sitting there in the hayloft that day, she couldn't help but wonder what kind of relationship existed between the two cats. Between the able-bodied one and the one who could not possibly forage for itself. It certainly wasn't a case of a mother cat bringing sustenance to her kittens. No, it was more complex than that. She said it suggested a degree of loyalty she wouldn't have thought cats capable of. Maybe this was one for the books. Live and learn. When she remembered that as recently as the day before, Paddy had contemplated shooting the white cat, she almost lost her composure.

"Shut the damn light off and let's get out of here," she said.

Paddy wasn't so sure. "What, and leave them up here?"

"Yes, leave them up here. What else? They don't need us. They've been getting along quite well without us. Unless you want to try catching them and take them to the Vet."

"Are you kidding?" Paddy said, scrambling after her down the ladder. "They'd have you in shreds. They're wild, for God's sake."

"Not as wild as you might think, my dear husband. From now on, I'm going to put food out for them. Next time I'm at Safeway, I'm going to lay in a supply of the best cat food they offer. I don't ever expect to tame those two, nor would it be a good idea. But if, after they learn to trust us, either of them decides they want to come inside, I'll hold the door open."

"You're not serious," Paddy said, brushing straw off himself as they headed for the house.

"Oh, but I am," Dodie said.

As Paddy would soon discover, and as I happen to know for a fact, she was.

Chapter Eleven

Tugboats Is My Life

My name is Boniface and I'm descended from a long line of Birmans. Birmans, in case you didn't know, supposedly originated in Burma a while back, where they were mainly the pets of Burmese high priests and lived in Burmese temples. I'm no racial supremacist, but I hate it when people confuse us with ordinary Burmese cats, those half-Tonkinese, half-Siamese hybrids who walk around with their noses in the air and their heads in the clouds. They couldn't catch a three-legged rat wearing cement shoes. They couldn't catch butterflies with a net. Neither could the Balinese, which, if you ask me, are nothing but long-haired Turks.

Anyway, after leaving Burma, some of my ancestors went to France and some went to England. The ones who went to France ended up intermarrying with the locals and produced a dissolute race of red cats. The others, the ones who went to England, mingled mostly with British shorthairs. Their offspring were either blue or chocolate. If what my late father told me is true, I myself am descended from this second group. Technically speaking, I'm a chocolate Birman. Or rather I would be, if it weren't for my maternal blood line. About that, the less said the better.

In short, I guess I'll have to settle for being fractionally Birman. Which is better than being zero-Birman, since the feature that distinguishes us is our sapphire eyes. In a crowd, you can pick us Birmans out by our peepers.

On my father's side, there's a long-standing tradition of seamanship, chiefly, though not exclusively, on tugboats. My great-great-great-grandfather, blue-eyed Bertie, was ship's cat aboard the harbour tug *James Whalen* from 1905 to 1916. As a matter of fact, he was aboard the *Whalen* on April 6, 1910 when the first wireless message ever sent from a Canadian ship crackled off her antenna. Though Bertie didn't live to see the *Whalen* converted to diesel, his son Boffo did, the same year the trusty old icebreaker was sent away to the East Coast, where she lived out the rest of her working life. They'd both be pleased to know the *Whalen* is back home now, tied up as a museum ship.

My great-great-grandfather, blue-eyed Boffo, was very briefly ship's cat aboard the trawler *Cerisoles*, which, as everyone knows, along with her sister ship *Inkerman*, sailed east from the Lakehead one day in 1918 and was never seen again. Some thought the two vessels might have struck Superior Shoal and sunk. Others thought they might have ventured forth from the Port Arthur Shipyard before they were sufficiently sea-worthy for Lake Superior. To this day, no one knows for certain what became of them. Maybe it was sabo-tage. Fortunately, great-great-grandfather Boffo, having had a premonition, as Birmans often do, vacated *Ceri-soles* on the eve of her departure and was thus spared a watery grave. When next he went to sea, it was aboard the slender wooden yacht *Sebastopol*, which had been built at Canada Car in Fort William. I'm not sure, but I think he finished out his career aboard the passenger steamer *South American*, a notoriously rat-ridden ship, sailing between Thunder Bay and Duluth.

My great-grandfather, blue-eyed Buster, was for several years ship's cat aboard the Canada Steamship Line's *Huronic*. He was aboard her the day Captain Mirrlees ran her aground on Lucile Island, opposite the mouth of the Pigeon River, in 1928. According to my father, the fastest vessel Buster ever sailed on was the *Huronic*'s sister ship, *Hamonic*, which once set a speed record between Thunder Bay and Sault Ste. Marie under the command of Captain Marx.

My grandfather, blue-eyed Boxer (thus named be-cause even as a kitten, and certainly as a young stud, he was forever challenging other cats to boxing matches) began his naval career on the tug *Thunder Cape*. Later he transferred to the *Peninsula*, then to the *Strathmore*. Back in those days, certain potent tugs towed rafts of logs from Nipigon to pulp mills in Thunder Bay, and Boxer served on those too. Every spring, at the opening of navigation, he'd leave his family in the catacombs under Saskatchewan Pool 6 and go down to the tugboat docks to see who needed a ship's cat. Of course, if the tug captains had a choice, they'd always pick a blue-eyed Birman. What they were looking for was first and foremost a good sailor, and after that a good ratter. If the cat was a good companion too, and never got sea-sick, and wasn't afraid of storms, and didn't get bored moving at half a mile an hour day after day with a heavy raft of logs behind, those were admirable qualities too.

Instead of cats, some tugboats took along dogs. But you seldom find a dog who, if he can catch rats in the bilge, can also keep mice out of the galley. Or if he can keep mice out of the galley, he's afraid of storms. Or if he isn't afraid of storms, he barks at inopportune times, such as when the tug is stealing boom logs from around somebody else's raft. Or if he doesn't bark at inopportune times, he can't stand being at sea, away from home, for eight months at a time. And there is always the problem of canine toilet facilities. Put bluntly, dogs are really stupid when it comes to heads, latrines and water closets. I mean, how many dogs have you ever seen using a litter box? They're too stupid. And if you're at sea for days, even weeks, at a stretch, as you're apt to be, what's a poor dog to do? Cross his legs and turn purple? I rest my case.

The way my father described it, every spring the tugboat captains, while their craft were being readied for service, would scan the year's crop of qualified cats. Some had their favourites from previous years. Word got around as to who was a good ratter, who was a big eater, who snuck ashore at every opportunity to visit the ladies and had to be summoned by four and a half blasts on the ship's whistle.

I know for a fact that family reputation counted for a lot. Because of blue-eyed Bertie's sterling credentials, blue-eyed Boffo, when his time came, had no trouble signing on. And because of Boffo's prowess, Buster was a shoo-in. And because of Buster's spotless record, Boxer could have had his choice of five or six boats. By the same token, his half-brothers, Uncle Basil and Uncle Beppo were snapped up by the *Robert W* and the *Rosalee D* respectively. My own father, blue-eyed Boris, could have signed on while still underage. As it was, he accompanied Boxer aboard the icebreaker *Alexander Henry* as an apprentice ship's cat two years before he was eligible. He was given light duties and catnip toys to play with, but by the end of the season was standing watch just like everyone else. Needless to say, blue-eyed Boxer was very proud of him. The following year, Boris was given full status aboard the lighthouse supply ship, *Montmorency*.

And so it was only natural that I continue in this ageless tradition of going down to the sea as a ship's cat. But don't get me wrong—I know it's not for everyone. My elder siblings, blue-eyed Bobby and blue-eyed Bruce, for example, when asked by my father a few seasons ago if they'd like him to put in a good word down at the tugboat dock, declined emphatically. Which was too bad. I think Papa was disappointed. There were openings that year aboard the *Robert John*, the *George N. Carleton* and the *Donald Mac*, but my brothers were not interested. At the time, we had just moved from the shadowy catacombs under Saskatchewan Pool 6 to a spacious upper suite of rooms in a recently abandoned silo, and they were unwilling to sacrifice the comfort of such lodgings for a summer on stormy Lake Superior. I remember my father saying, "But it's a family tradition. It goes back five generations. And then there's the camaraderie." And Bobby saying, "What, bouncing around in a dirty, noisy tugboat, chasing rats in the bilges, listening to the roar of the engine day and night, never being able to walk on solid ground from April till December? You call that a life? No, thank you. We'll stay ashore with mother and Boniface and live like civilized cats."

I well remember the hurt in my father's eyes. They might as well have told him they had no respect for his chosen profession, nor for the contribution he was making to the shipping industry. I think their attitude wounded him deeply. I'm not sure he ever fully recovered.

A few days later, Boris was taken aboard the *Point Valour* for the season and we didn't see him again until Christmas Eve. He and the *Valour* spent the summer assisting saltwater vessels in and out of port, towing them from elevator to elevator, turning them in the slips, transporting pilots back and forth. When he came ashore he told us how kind the *Valour*'s crew had been to him, giving him a nice warm nook in the engine room for his bed, lined with blankets, and a special shelf in the wheelhouse on which he could recline during the day when not patrolling the pantry. He became special friends with Captain Leckham, chief engineer Benchley and first mate Blofeld, and though he didn't catch many mice, he said it was one of the best seasons he'd ever spent. Unfortunately, he came down with a chill that winter in the defunct elevator, and before we knew it, his chill had turned into pneumonia. We did all we could for him, but in spite of everything, he passed away at the end of March.

So blue-eyed Boris is gone now, off to join all those other blue-eyed Birmans at the big tugboat harbour in the sky. Gone, but not forgotten. I understand there's a colour photo of him on the office wall at Thunder Bay Marine Services Ltd., down by the ore trestle. As well, there's a portrait of Grampa Boxer down at the office of Gravel & Lake Services on Dock #5, with the inscription: "Blue-eyed Boxer, faithful friend and ship's cat extraordinaire. Ne plus ultra." Which seems appropriate, since, in Greek mythology, those last three words also appear on the mariners' memorial at the Pillars of Hercules. I've heard via the grapevine that shipping agent Sokolov plans to commission small clay statues of Boxer and Boris to grace his foyer on Main Street.

My own first assignment as ship's cat was aboard the harbour tug *Coastal Cruiser*, and I'm sure Captain Bray chose me because of my father's reputation, and his father's before him, and his father's before that. The moment I stepped aboard I knew it was the life for me. I felt it in my heart and in my nose. When the aroma of hot oil hit my nostrils, I felt I'd come home. I could almost see Boris peering over my shoulder, saying, "Well done, son." And behind him, Boffo and Bertie and Buster, all smiles, happy in the knowledge that the tradition was continuing. I'm sure Captain Bray understood this. And as we bobbed about the harbour, our engine roaring, our pennants snapping in the breeze, I think he was happy to have his tug in such good hands. That summer, we voyaged as far as Silver Islet and Isle Royale, once even to Point Porphry Lighthouse. We transported adventurers, geologists and scuba divers. Everywhere we went, people said how glad they were to see the *Coastal Cruiser* flying from her masthead the burgee that indicates, "Ship's Cat on Board." It's the swallow-tailed flag bearing the likeness of a blue-eyed

Birman, right above the white one that indicates, "Pilot on Board." Next time you're at Marina Park on a summer's day, or over at Keefer Terminal, or down on Dock #5, maybe you'll keep an eye out for it. It's the same flag that was flying from the mast of the *Glenada* that stormy October night in 1996, when the brave tugboat went out into the teeth of a terrible gale and rescued the stricken pleasure craft, *Grampa Woo*. On that occasion, as was reported in Reader's Digest, Captain Gerry Dawson, his engineer, Jack Olson, his first mate, Jim Harding, and his ship's cat, my cousin Bram, all received commendations for bravery.

Chapter Twelve

Armadillo & The Curmudgeon

The first meeting between Armadillo, the cat, and cranky old Mr. Honneger, did not go well. At the time, Mr. Honneger had been a resident of Bethany Retirement Home for several years. His only living relative was a nephew in Nova Scotia, so he never had visitors. All his working life he'd been a Customs Officer at the Pigeon River border, with a reputation for being fierce and thorough and unswerving in his duty. His great delight was to catch people with undeclared merchandise and threaten to arrest them for smuggling. He would rant and rave, promise lengthy jail terms, demand the keys to their cars. It was not uncommon for him to make women cry and grown men tremble.

Mr. Honneger spent his days at Bethany in the sun room, watching T.V., reading Ian Fleming novels, doing crossword puzzles. Because he was so gruff and uncommunicative, people tended to leave him alone. If they spoke to him at all, they only wished him Good Morning, or commented on the weather, especially if it was cold and damp out, because like many of them, Mr. Honneger suffered from stiffness. As often as not, all he did was harrumph and go on with his reading. His fellow-pensioners soon gave up asking him to play bingo or join a cribbage tournament. If he accompanied them on an outing to Boulevard Lake or Old Fort William, he'd sit by himself at the back of the bus and stare out the window. On Christmas Day, he remained in his room, emerging only to eat his turkey dinner. He took no part in carol singing or tree decorating. He neither gave nor received presents. Behind his back, his colleagues called him Scrooge. If Mr. Honneger heard them, as he must have, he gave no sign. He went shuffling off down the hall in his cardigan and bedroom slippers, seemingly unneedful of anyone's company, even at Christmas. And though some of the oldtimers felt sorry for him, deplored his inability to socialize, most of them just shrugged their shoulders and shook their heads. If he was lonely, it was his own fault, because Bethany was known for its friendliness.

Take, for example, Gilda Coneybear's striped grey cat, Armadillo. Three afternoons a week, little Gilda would hurry home from school, put Armadillo in his basket, and carry him down the street to Bethany Retirement Home. The reason she'd named him Armadillo, by the way, was because even as a kitten, and more so as he aged, the dark stripes on his fur made him appear decked out in layers of armour plate. Though Gilda had never encountered a real armadillo, she'd seen a picture of one on the Internet, with its short legs and pointed face, and was struck by her cat's similarity, especially when he crouched and put his rump in the air, ready to pounce.

Armadillo's job at Bethany was to walk around and entertain. From the start, he seemed not only to understand this, but to enjoy it. He would visit people in the sun room, allow himself to be stroked and patted and told how handsome he was, despite his superficial resemblance to an armour-plated, burrowing rodent. He would stretch and roll over on his back, and let people prod his tummy. He would jump into the laps of old ladies in wheelchairs, and he gave equal attention to people confined to bed. Gilda would follow him from room to room as he made his rounds, making sure he didn't eat too many treats, steering him away from those patients who disliked cats. Some days he even wandered into the spa, paraded around the rim of the hot tub with his tail in the air, peering through the mist at wrinkled octogenarians taking the waters.

It must be said that Mr. Honneger was not fond of cats. Neither was he fond of dogs, except perhaps old basset hounds who had lost their voices. The first time he laid eyes on Armadillo, he was watching T.V. in the sun room. Weekday afternoons he liked to observe

Judge Mills Lane deal severely with underhanded defendants, berating them, cutting them down to size, as they so rightly deserved. On one such afternoon, he looked up and saw Gilda standing in the doorway, and at her feet, Armadillo, scrutinizing him, as though trying to decide whether he was friend or foe.

"What the hell is that?" Mr. Honneger said, glowering.

"That's my cat," Gilda said. "I bring him here to cheer up the residents. His name is Armadillo."

Mr. Honneger made a sour face. "That's a stupid name for a cat. Why would you call him that?"

"Because in a certain light, his markings look like scales."

"No, they don't."

"He has short legs, a skinny tail, a narrow face."

"Well, I agree with you, he's ugly. He might just be the ugliest cat I've ever seen. But he doesn't look like an armadillo. What's he doing here, anyway? This is no place for a cat. Cats carry germs and shed fur. I'm allergic to cats. They're sneaky. They kill birds. They dig up your garden, shred your curtains. I thought we had rules. I thought animals weren't allowed. If I were you, I'd get that ugly cat out of here before anyone sees him. Otherwise, you'll be in big trouble, young lady."

"But I have permission, sir," Gilda said. "Armadillo's been invited to visit residents who don't mind his presence."

Mr. Honneger bristled, wagged his finger. "Is that so? Well, I do mind his presence, and I say get him the hell out of here before I whack him with a magazine. Sneaky creature, spreading germs. And where does he do his business? Not under my bed, I hope. I intend to check the regulations."

For Mr. Honneger, that was a long speech. Indeed, it was the longest speech he'd made since taking up residence at Bethany. As for Armadillo, he did an unexpected thing. He walked over to Mr. Honneger and rubbed his head against the old man's leg, as though happy to see him, as though they were friends. Then he departed, went down the hall to continue his rounds, leaving Mr. Honneger open-mouthed, either with surprise or disapproval.

On every visitation after that, inexplicably, Armadillo seemed to seek out Mr. Honneger. Not that he neglected his other commitments, but every Monday, Wednesday and Friday, he looked for him in the sun room. If he wasn't there, the search continued in the dining room, in the card room, and down every corridor. And finally, if all else failed, in Mr. Honneger's room itself, where Armadillo would rush in, swishing his tail, chirping a greeting. Invariably, Mr. Honneger would say to Gilda, "Get your damn cat away from me. I hate cats. How many times do I have to tell you?"

"Well," Gilda would say, "I'm sorry, sir, but Armadillo likes you. I don't know why, but he does. He won't leave without seeing you and saying hello."

"That's ridiculous."

"Yes, I suppose it is, but what can I do?"

"Do you get paid to bring that damn cat in here?"

"Of course not. We do it voluntarily, because we like to."

"There should be rules. We need rules to protect our rights. Civilized society is run by rules and regulations. If I don't want visits from your cat, I shouldn't have to put up with them."

Gilda raised her arms in a gesture of helplessness. "But he's only a cat, sir. He doesn't know about rules.

And he likes you. He'd be very disappointed if he missed seeing you."

"Harrumph," Mr. Honneger said, but Gilda noticed that this time he didn't draw back when Armadillo gave him a farewell rub on the leg. It may have been her imagination, but she thought he almost reached down to touch the cat, then caught himself in time, and pretended to be distracted by noises from the music room.

From that day forward, according to Gilda, Armadillo worked on Mr. Honneger. He used all his coyness, all his seductive charm, like a smitten lover, perhaps seeing this as a challenge, seemingly determined to make a conquest. It wasn't long before his intended victim, the recipient of his attention, quit trying to hide from him. Every Monday, Wednesday and Friday afternoon, Mr. Honneger would be in the sun room, waiting. One day, deeming the time ripe, Armadillo casually jumped into Mr. Honneger's lap, gave him a brazen rub on the chin, tickled his ear with his whiskers. Before Mr. Honneger could react, Armadillo curled up and lay down, with his paws folded sedately under him. There, in the sun, with everyone watching and smiling at his obvious seduction, Armadillo closed his eyes and commenced to purr loudly. Poor Mr. Honneger. Debauched, as it were, his honour stained. There wasn't much he could do except stroke Armadillo's back and scratch him behind the ears, which of course produced an even louder purr. Soon, in fact, purring filled the room, and people said what a great lion tamer Mr. Honneger would have made, with his innate understanding of felines. Some of them professed jealousy, because despite coaxing and the offer of tidbits filched from the dining room, Armadillo had never rewarded them with such a show of affection, with such loud, passionate purring.

"You definitely have a way with cats, Mr. Honneger," they said.

Which made the old man smile. Gilda Coneybear smiled too. So did sly Armadillo. Because they all knew it was really the other way around. It was Armadillo who had done the courting, the flirting, and was now reaping his reward. Maybe it's true: the toughest nut to crack is often the tastiest.

Chapter Thirteen

The Cuban Cat

It had not been a good year for Louella. As a matter of fact, it had been a terrible year. For one thing, she'd been cut loose from her job as assistant producer at the radio station. After fifteen years, she'd fallen victim to what they called down-sizing. More accurately, she'd been replaced by someone younger and more enlightened, a girl barely out of high school, who was more in touch with today's trends, and who, starting at the bottom, had come on board at half Louella's salary.

For another thing, Louella and her husband Herb, after harsh words, counselling and more harsh words, had agreed to separate. It had been a stormy marriage at best. That they'd stayed together this long had been more a matter of obstinacy than compatibility. Ironically, their friends thought they made an ideal couple, when in truth, almost from the beginning, they'd been at each other's throats. The fact that Herb had a drinking problem and was away from home so much, in his capacity as regional franchise facilitator for Kentucky Fried Chicken, had not helped. Nor had the fact that as he emerged on the wrong side of forty he tended to scoff at the antiquated notion of marital fidelity. "That's an old fashioned concept," he was fond of saying. "These days, people play the field. The poet was right, you know: 'The grave's a fine and private place, but none I fear do there embrace.'"

Fortunately, their two sons, Kyle and Kevin, were both away at college, Kyle at Concordia, studying art, Kevin at Ryerson, hoping to become a journalist. Both boys were industrious, independent, and worked at Kentucky Fried Chicken outlets in their respective cities. They had inherited their father's charm and good looks, their mother's creativity, and except for occasional requests for money and brushes with the law, were no trouble to anyone.

What had made this a particularly bad year for Louella was the death of her beloved cat, Natasha, a devoted Russian blue, who, at the age of nineteen, had succumbed to the ravages of old age and expired on Valentine's Day.

Next morning Louella went down to Thunder Country Travel and expressed her desire to fly south to some nice warm beach in the Caribbean, where she'd find a quiet, inexpensive seaside hotel, with palm trees and good music, but not too many people.

"I suppose that's impossible," she said.

"No," her travel agent said. "That's cool. That's possible. These days, that's Cuba. To be specific, the Posada Los Alamos, on the Atlantic side, in the coastal town of Nuevitas. There you'll find everything you've just mentioned, plus good rum and good cigars. A day's bus ride from Havana, two hours from Santiago." And so that's where Louella went. All by herself. It was the first time she'd gone anywhere in years, and certainly the first time unaccompanied.

She got off the plane at Camaguey airport and took the shuttle bus to Nuevitas. Sitting next to her was a bald, sunburnt American from Casper, Wyoming, a Mr. Chaffey, who owned a chain of stores that sold nothing but Wrangler jeans. He said he'd spent his holidays last year in Jamaica, at Montego Bay, and had visited Ian Fleming's house, where the James Bond novels were written. He said the only way he could enter Cuba now was on a foreign plane. Next year, he said, he intended to spend his two weeks in the Bahamas, probably at Nassau, where he planned to further his study of voodoo. Would Louella be interested, he wanted to know, in exploring Havana with him, hiring a cab to see the sights, helping him arrange to smuggle out a few boxes of cigars? He said he'd recently seen a Ry Cooder film called *The Buena Vista Social Club*, all about old Havana and its beloved musicians, and he wanted to hear more of their music.

But Louella said no, she didn't think so, because her husband, a high-ranking RCMP officer, would be joining her at the Posada Los Alamos, and he was a real stickler for propriety. Not only that, she said, James Bond couldn't hold a candle to him when it came to sniffing out skulduggery.

Louella's first impression of the Posada Los Alamos was that it had probably seen better days. It was older and seedier than she'd imagined, and so were most of the guests, none of whom, she soon discovered, was Cuban. But the staff was friendly, her room bright and airy, and from her balcony she could look down at the beach and feel the wind off the ocean. There was a tiled swimming pool in the courtyard, surrounded by palm trees and bougainvillea, with plastic chairs under umbrellas and a scattering of stone chess tables at which somnolent old men in shirt sleeves were seated.

But it was the somewhat dilapidated dining room that attracted her, with its ceiling fans and tall windows facing the sea. There, that first day at lunch, she discovered a large party of elderly German tourists, another of Japanese, yet another of Canadians, and of course Mr. Chaffey, the Wrangler salesman from Wyoming, who invited her to sit at his table.

"I don't seem to see your husband," he said, already perspiring in the unaccustomed humidity.

Louella shook her head, sipped her welcoming glass of champagne. "No, he's been unavoidably detained in Puerto Rico. There was a message waiting for me. He'll come as soon as he can."

Mr. Chaffey gave her a comforting look, possibly tinged with disbelief. "Of course. As soon as he can."

Sensing his incredulity, Louella wondered why she was lying. Did she expect to keep up the RCMP myth indefinitely? Was it some sort of shield? Was it because she'd taken an instant dislike to pathetic Mr.

Chaffey? At the same time, there was something in-
triguing about a man who sold bluejeans for a living
and went about the Caribbean studying voodoo. All in
all, she wondered whether it might have been easier to
tell him the truth, because this way, like James Bond,
she'd need to be on her toes and remember exactly
what she'd said.

"Do you have children?" he asked, starting in on his
fish paste sandwiches.

"Yes. Two grown boys. Both at university."

"And do they expect to pursue careers in law
enforcement?"

"Law enforcement? Good heavens, no. Why on
earth would they?"

"Well, with your husband being in the Mounted
Police. I assume he rides a horse and always gets his
man?"

Fortunately, at that moment, they were distracted by
the arrival of a large, bluish cat with luminous amber
eyes. Louella was so surprised, and yet so pleased, to
see a cat in a hotel dining room, that she nearly
knocked over her glass of champagne. "Oh, look, Mr.
Chaffey," she said, pointing at the cat as it approached
their table, fixing them with its stare. "Have you ever
seen such a handsome, gorgeous creature?"

Mr. Chaffey smiled, motioned the waiter for refills.
"Truthfully, I haven't. Are you a cat fancier?"

"I am, indeed. Until recently, I owned a blue cat. Her
name was Natasha. I had her for nineteen years. If I
didn't know better, I'd say she'd been reincarnated here
on the island of Cuba. Although now that I take a closer
look, I think she was a shade darker than this one, and
her eyes weren't so orange."

"Copper," Mr. Chaffey said. "Unless I'm mistaken,

this is a Lilac Burmese, and they have copper or chartreuse eyes, but not orange. I believe they're fairly
common in the West Indies. I've certainly seen them in
Jamaica. Ian Fleming owned a pair, as did his friend,
Noel Coward. I like cats too. My late mother, rest her
soul, used to breed them. She attended all the important
shows, won a few prizes. Her specialty was the Cornish
Rex. Later she became a judge. I've had at least a
dozen cats over the years, but never anything so exotic
as a Lilac Burmese. I believe this one coming toward
us has his mind on handouts."

Which it did. After being shooed away by the table
of Germans, and after one of the Japanese ladies had
stamped her foot at it, the Lilac Burmese came and sat
beside Louella. It looked up at her with its unblinking
copper eyes and laid a front paw gently against her
ankle. Very softly, so softly as to be almost inaudible,
it then emitted the faintest of meows, a plaintive, plead-
ing sound, as though it were on the verge of starvation.
Which it clearly was not.

Mr. Chaffey, looking down from his side of the
table, extracted the fish paste filling from a dainty
sandwich and slipped it unobtrusively to the cat, who
licked it off his finger. "It seems to me," he said, "this
cat has developed a technique for mooching."

"My Natasha used to do the same thing," Louella
said.

"But not in the dining room of a tourist hotel. Where
I come from, in the United States, it wouldn't be
allowed."

Louella began taking the filling out of her sandwiches too, and passing it down to the now purring
Lilac Burmese. "Isn't it nice," she said, "to know there
are places in the world where rules are relaxed, where

people can be themselves, where cats are free to come and go as they please. I think it's marvelous. If I owned a hotel, I'd have it full of cats, and people who disapproved could go somewhere else."

Just then the waiter approached with a fresh bottle of champagne and more fishy sandwiches. On his lapel he wore a tag with the name Antonio on it.

"Antonio," Mr. Chaffey said, "does your hotel allow cats in the dining room?"

Antonio shook his head vigorously. "No, senor, these cat and these dog are no allow in these dining room. They are also no allow in these kitchen. The only place the dog and the cat are allow eez in these bedroom. Eef you bring these dog and these cat with you. Or, eef one wander in from these garden and wish to visit you, and you don' mind, then they can visit you. But in these dining room, senor, eez no allow. Too many people don' like these dog and these cat. Maybe in Habana eez different, but here at Posada Los Alamos, eez ver' strict."

"Just as I thought," Mr. Chaffey said, holding out his champagne glass for a refill. "Thank you, Antonio."

Which made Louella smile, because all the time they'd been talking, the Lilac Burmese cat with the copper eyes had been in plain view, sitting at her feet, licking fish paste off her finger.

"De nada," Antonio said, laughing, wandering off to pour champagne at the other tables.

"Mr. Chaffey," Louella said, "I'm afraid I have a confession to make. My husband isn't an officer in the RCMP. He's a franchise facilitator for Kentucky Fried Chicken. He and I are separated. He's not in Puerto Rico. I have no idea where he is. One thing for sure, he's not coming here."

Mr. Chaffey looked at her, clinked his champagne glass against hers. "Well, now," he said. "Well, now. Imagine that."

"And may I say something else? I'd be happy to visit Havana with you. We might even find the Buena Vista Social Club and listen to some of that Cuban music you spoke about. I'd also like to go for a swim, and walk on the beach, and have lunch under the palm trees. I'd especially like to invite this beautiful blue cat to my room for the night, if he'll come. Do you by any chance play chess?"

Mr. Chaffey shook his head sadly. "No, I'm afraid I don't."

"Thank God. Neither do I. Nor do I play tennis."

Mr. Chaffey shrugged, guffawed, signalled Antonio for more champagne. "I'm afraid we're out of sandwiches too," he said, indicating the naked slices of bread, from which all the fish paste filling had been scraped.

Chapter Fourteen

Mungo Park, Cat-About-Town

Mungo Park is another of those cats whose origins are obscure. All that can be said for certain is that he possesses the coloration, ego and personality of a Burmese, but not the pedigree. Were he of noble birth, his coat might be described as tangerine, his eyes chartreuse. But being a down-to-earth kind of guy, there's a good chance he'd pooh-pooh these descriptions.

Among his owners he counts the Tilbury family,

who live on Secord Street, a block from Cornwall School. The youngest Tilbury child, a red-headed boy named Adam, when asked one night at dinner what he'd learned in school that day, announced that a pumpkin-coloured kitten had wandered into his eighth grade classroom, right in the middle of a spelling-bee, and that the teacher, Miss Huphnagel, hadn't even noticed. Though this was a true story, nobody at the dinner table that night believed him, partly because he had a habit of inventing, partly because they were too busy listening to his sister, Hermione. And so next day, to impress everyone, he brought the pumpkin-coloured kitten home with him. When his father asked him what he'd learned in school that day, he said not a word, but captured everyone's attention by placing the cat in the middle of the table.

"What the hell is that?" his father asked.

"That's a cat, dear," Mrs. Tilbury said.

"I know it's a cat, but where the hell did it come from?"

"It wandered into school," Adam said. "So I brought it home with me."

"Well, my boy, you can damn well take it back again. We'll have no stray cats in this house."

While his mother dished out bread pudding and treacle for dessert, Adam held the cat on his lap and fed it morsels of poached salmon scavenged from dirty dinner plates. That night he took it to bed with him, let it sleep under the covers, and at breakfast, behind his father's back, gave it the milk off his porridge.

Though it was a male cat, Adam decided to name it Vivian, after Miss Huphnagel, his grade eight teacher at Cornwall School. When he told his mother, she smiled. When he told his sister, Hermione, she laughed and called him an idiot. No cat, she said, not even a pumpkin-coloured cat, was ever called Vivian. Cats were named Spot, or Fluffy, or Tiger, but not Vivian. And so then and there, to avoid further humiliation, Adam changed the cat's name to Spike, which was what he called an imaginary brother who sometimes came to cheer him when he was sick in bed.

If Adam expected loyalty from Spike, he was due for disappointment. At that stage in his life, Spike was not a one-person cat. Besides, he had the wanderlust. No sooner had Adam's father relented and said he could keep him, than Spike set off for parts unknown. Mrs. Tilbury let him out the back door one morning after Adam had left for school, and he did not come back. At least he did not come back right away. A week later, he wandered nonchalantly into Miss Huphnagel's class at Cornwall School again. Only this time she saw him. "Whose cat is that?" she asked sharply. "Does anyone own this cat?"

Adam waited a moment, then raised his hand. "It's my cat," he said. "His name is Spike."

Naturally, the class tittered. Miss Huphnagel frowned and hunched her shoulders, as she usually did when vexed. "Adam Tilbury, you cannot bring your cat to school. You should know that. Where do you live?"

"I live on Secord Street, ma'am."

"Then will you please take Spike home and deposit him there, and at four o'clock you can make up the lost time by cleaning my blackboards for me."

So that's what Adam did. He picked Spike up and carried him home, and was so glad to see him that he never thought of scolding him for running away. Not that the cat appeared to have suffered. His coat was clean, he looked well fed, and around his neck he wore a nice new flea collar. Though it caused Adam pain, his mother said she wondered if maybe Spike was leading a double life.

And of course, he was. A double, triple, quadruple life. For the next several years, that was to be his *modus operandi*. He would stay with the Tilburys a week or two, sometimes as long as a month, enjoying their hospitality, sleeping on Adam's bed, then disappear for the same length of time. During his absences, they saw neither hide nor hair of him. Usually when he returned, besides being a little fatter, he would be freshly combed and coiffed. His claws would have been clipped, his ears cleaned. Mr. Tilbury said it was the damnedest thing he'd ever heard of, sharing a cat with God knows how many other people. "It's nonsensical!" he used to say, every time Spike showed up at the door from one of his furloughs.

But Mrs. Tilbury only smiled and remembered a footloose ex-boyfriend of hers, dashing Renzo Shiaparelli, who had done the very same thing back in her courting days. Where was he now? she wondered.

The same year Adam went away to the Ontario College of Art in Toronto, Miss Huphnagel's nephew, Professor Phillpotts, came to town as chair of the geography department at Lakehead University.

After a good deal of searching, Professor Phillpotts and his wife, Henrietta, found a nice bungalow to rent on Ambrose Street, two blocks west of Secord. It was closely surrounded by trembling aspens, and directly behind it rose the steep embankment that culminates in Hillcrest Park. With help from Creekside Nursery, the Phillpotts were able to plant rose bushes and honeysuckle vines, even some English ivy and a dwarf persimmon tree.

While the professor was away at work all day, teaching his eager young students all about famous African explorers, such as Richard Burton, Mungo Park and David Livingston, Mrs. Phillpotts stayed at home and practised her calligraphy. Hour after hour, day after day, she sat by the open kitchen window, covering sheets of paper with epigrams and aphorisms, lines from Tennyson, whole verses from the Bible. She always said that when she got good enough, she'd turn her talent to some useful purpose, such as plaques or greeting cards. But her husband had begun to wonder if she ever would. She'd been practising for ten years now, but felt confident only up to the letter "Q" in Gothic script.

For amusement, the Phillpotts liked to get in their car and drive to southern Ontario, or northern Michigan, or even Wisconsin. When they went away on holiday, they often towed a camper, which they would set up every night and sleep in. Professor Phillpotts said that such expeditions made him feel heroic, like the intrepid African explorers he so admired. He wore canvas boots, short pants, a safari jacket with many pockets, a khaki pith helmet. He always had binoculars around his neck, and a telephoto lens on his camera. His wife, while happy enough, didn't completely share his enthusiasm, because on the road she couldn't practise her calligraphy.

If Professor Phillpotts had a quirk, it was his fear of having his house burglarized while he was away. To forestall this, he put bars on the windows and heavy padlocks on both doors. He left the lights on and the radio playing. He cancelled the mail and the newspaper. He asked his neighbour across the street, Mrs. von Steuben, who seldom left her front porch, to keep an eye on things. You would have thought these precautions would be enough.

But they weren't.

One year in August, upon returning from the bushveld of northern Minnesota, the Phillpotts unlocked their front door and discovered a full-grown, pumpkin-coloured cat curled up on the living room couch. At first, Professor Phillpotts was dumbfounded. Then angry. Then perplexed. The doors had been securely locked. There was no sign of forced entry. Nor, at a quick glance, did anything seem to be missing. The radio was still playing. The lights were still on. As he stood there open-mouthed, the cat, who looked well cared for and was wearing a flea collar, got up and stretched. Though not what you could call hostile, it appeared to be glowering, as who wouldn't be, when intruders barge in and disturb your sleep?

Mrs. Phillpotts said, "Good heavens, dear, how do you suppose that cat got in here?"

Professor Phillpotts, who had been wondering the same thing, clapped his hands together and cried, "Shoo!"

But the cat was in no hurry to leave. It stepped down off the couch, began washing its face. Next it sauntered into the kitchen. Then it jumped up on Mrs. Phillpotts' calligraphy table, from there to the window sill, and finally out the open window and into the branches of a trembling aspen.

"Who left that damn window open?" the Professor wanted to know.

Henrietta lifted her chin. "Perhaps I did, dear. I like to have fresh air while I practise my letters. I find it keeps my head clear."

"Well, just see what you've done with your stupid

open-window policy? You've allowed a stray cat to take up residence. Your head wasn't so clear after all."

Which made Henrietta bristle. "I hardly think it's taken up residence. It certainly hasn't been eating here. Only sleeping on the couch. And really, dear, you're the one who's stupid. You were so preoccupied with padlocking the doors that you never thought to make sure the windows were closed before we left for Minnesota. And while we're on the subject, may I say I'm getting a bit tired of these stupid junkets we keep going on, sleeping in a stupid tent, cooking on a stupid camp stove. I believe after this I'll stay home and do my stupid calligraphy."

Later that day, Professor Phillpotts calmed down and apologized to his wife. Things could have been worse, he said. Had it wanted to, the cat could have made a real mess. It could have torn up the furniture and sprayed the walls. All it had done, judging by the tell-tale pumpkin-coloured fur they found, was sleep on the couch and on their bed. It must, he said, have been a considerate, well behaved animal, much like the cats he'd owned as a boy. Were it to return, he said, he'd have no qualms about letting it in.

Mrs. van Steuben across the street, taking credit for having guarded the house so well, said yes, she'd seen a large, pumpkin-coloured cat climbing the trembling aspens. She'd assumed it was after birds. Did she know whose cat it was? Well, no, but she'd seen it often enough, prowling the neighbourhood. She thought it looked like a Burmese.

Spike's story might end there, and the puzzle might never have been solved, had Henrietta Phillpotts not found herself in young Adam Tilbury's evening calligraphy class last spring at the 55 Plus Centre on River Street. Though they lived only a few blocks apart, they'd never previously met. Adam said the first thing he noticed was Henrietta's exceptional skill. Especially her proficiency in Gothic script. Even he couldn't make a better Q.

One evening after class, Henrietta invited him to her house for coffee. Imagine his surprise when he walked in and saw Spike asleep on the living room couch.

"Is that your cat?" he asked.

Which made Henrietta chuckle. "Well, not exactly," she said. "I don't know whose it is. When we came home from one of our expeditions, we found it on the couch, right where it is now. It had come in through the kitchen window. At first, my husband was angry and chased it away. But next day it was back, meowing at the door, and since we both like cats, and since it's quite handsome and very clean, we let it in and fed it. Ever since, it thinks it lives here. Although sometimes it disappears for days on end. We have no idea where it goes. I expect it has a good home somewhere nearby. Someone obviously takes care of it when it's not with us. It always has a nice new flea collar on. We named it Mungo Park, after my husband's favourite African explorer. He's become very attached to it and gets quite upset if it stays away too long."

Taking his coffee with him, Adam went and sat beside Spike on the couch. He stroked his pumpkin-coloured fur, scratched him behind the ears. "Mungo Park, you say? What a strange name for a cat. But perhaps it suits him. I once had a kitten named Vivian, but my sister made me change it to Spike."

At which, if what Adam says is true, and I see no

reason to doubt him, Mungo Park opened his eyes wide and let out a meow of recognition.

"Cats are mysterious, aren't they?" Henrietta said. "I believe they keep secrets. You certainly have a way with them. A person would think the two you were old friends."

Chapter Fifteen

Renée & Racine: French Cats

R enée and Racine belong to Madame Béziers, who lives in La Rochelle, a seaport on the west coast of France. The three of them inhabit a spacious, but old-fashioned apartment on the seventh floor of a building that overlooks La Rochelle Harbour. From her balcony, Madame Béziers has a splendid view of the two 14th-century stone towers that guard the entrance to the inner basin. During slave-trading days, when La Rochelle was a jump-off point for the West Indies and the New World, chains were stretched across between these two ancient towers to prevent slave ships from departing before taxes and duties had been collected

133

and import-export fees paid. Even in those days, business was business.

In La Rochelle's famed Musée du Nouveau Monde on rue Fleuriau, where Madame Béziers worked for many years as curator, you can see old ledgers that were kept by the slave brokers. They show details of transactions, names of ships and their captains, overseas destinations, profit margins. No refunds for wormy biscuit, rough seas or last minute changes to itinerary. No reimbursement for pain, starvation or death. Expenses were kept to a minimum. In terms of raw numbers, it's apparent that slave-trading was a lucrative enterprise. Fortunes were made on both sides of the Atlantic. The shuttling of human cargo from Africa to La Rochelle to the U.S.A. never failed to turn a profit. The only fly in the ointment, it seems, was not conscience, but piracy. A section of the museum is devoted to that worthy profession too.

Madame Béziers, a short, plump, good-humoured lady, is a widow whose husband, a civil servant and part-time school teacher, died of a stroke at the age of fifty-seven. She herself studied library science at the Sorbonne, and later, after the war, at Selwyn College, Cambridge. She and Monsieur Béziers had three sons, all of whom went to the bustling city of Nantes, at the mouth of the Loire River, and found work as shipbuilders. Something I didn't know until recently was that they also had a daughter, whose name was Yvette, and who, because of severe mental illness, was committed to the Vincennes insane asylum on the outskirts of Paris when she was only fifteen.

Waking up one day and finding herself alone, Madame Béziers took a seventh-floor apartment in La Rochelle's old town, went back to work at the Musée du Nouveau Monde, and from an ailing sister-in-law inherited a white poodle and a brindled tabby cat. These animals already had names, but Madame Béziers changed them. She called the dog Renée (which of course means reborn), and the cat Racine, after her favourite 17th-century French dramatist, Jean Baptiste Racine, author of such classic tragedies as *Phèdre* and *Bérénice*. Before daughter Yvette was committed at Vincennes, Madame Béziers used to read Racine's plays to her, taking all the parts herself if her sons and husband were not in the mood. Evidently it was the one thing that calmed the child and made her manageable.

I must admit, when I first met Madame Béziers, at cocktails in her apartment with mutual friends, I was surprised to find her dog and cat living harmoniously under the same roof. At the time, I knew of no other such arrangement. These two animals didn't merely tolerate each other, they slept together, ate together, went for car rides in the back seat of Madame Béziers' Deux Chevaux convertible together. The evening of the cocktail party, they sat side by side on a chintz settee by the window, unobtrusively accepting tidbits. I myself fed them half my fancy canapés.

Another time, when I was at Madame Béziers apartment for dinner and the main course was coq de bruyère, I slipped them both generous portions under the table and let them lick the grease off my fingers. All the time I was doing it, I had the feeling my hostess knew exactly what I was up to.

Madame Béziers will tell you herself that her love for cars and car rides stems from her father, a rural veterinarian. Though she was only six years old when war broke out and he went off to fight in the Resistance, she remembers going for car rides with him in the vicinity of Angoulême, where they lived. On summer days they would pack a picnic lunch and drive through the verdant countryside, visiting farms and vineyards, and while her father tended to sick cows and sheep and horses, sometimes pigs, sometimes geese, sometimes dogs and cats, she would tag along behind, the envy of children her own age, who marvelled at her father's power to heal. She watched him give injections, sew up wounds, help ewes with difficult births. Every so often he had to put an ailing animal to sleep, and though he and the farmers would be stoic, she herself would often cry.

It's evident she adored her father, felt safe and secure in his presence. Because she was his youngest child and only daughter, she received and basked in much love and attention. She could think of no finer existence than driving through the province of Poitou-Charentes with him, sometimes as far north as the Loire Valley, sometimes as far south as Bordeaux, listening to him talk and sing and tell her she was the prettiest girl in all of France.

After the war started, she saw him rarely. Some nights he would come home, dirty and tired, and leave before morning. And then one cold, drizzly winter's day in 1943, her mother came to school and took her home and told her that her father, along with a dozen other Resistance fighters, had been executed by German soldiers at Limoges.

Though Madame Béziers seldom talks about it, over a glass of iced vermouth on the sidewalk at Café Gasconne, she will tell you she vividly remembers that winter's day in 1943, and the numb shock that ended her childhood and lasted for years.

Nowadays, with her husband laid to rest, her sons off in Nantes building ships, her daughter, who no longer recognizes anyone, locked away at Vincennes, Madame Béziers is back once again driving the backroads of Poitou-Charentes. She says things haven't changed all that much since the war. Oh, the cities and towns within driving distance of La Rochelle, with their factories and highrises, are more crowded, more congested. But she mostly avoids them. The countryside, she says, the orchards, the vineyards, are pretty much the same. Though the farmers from her father's era are gone, their sons and grandsons have taken over. It's true that one sees more tractors than oxen now, more cars, more school buses. But the cows and horses look the same, as do the spring lambs and domestic geese.

These sojourns in her little Deux Chevaux, she says, with the top down and the wind in her face, would be lonely without the company of Renée and Racine. Just as she loved going for car rides with her father, so her dog and cat seem to love accompanying her. As soon as they see her putting bread and cheese and fruit and a bottle of Beaujolais in her picnic basket, and when she dons her driving cap and sunglasses, they show signs of excitement. This may be evidenced by nothing more than sitting patiently at the door, watching her, but for Renée and Racine, that in itself is a departure from their normal routine of napping round the clock. It's true that on summer days they like to take their ease out on the balcony, where they sniff the air and listen to the cries of sea birds, but usually, when not attending cocktail parties, they sleep.

There is one other activity they enjoy too, and that is

going by car to the Café Gasconne on rue Talmont, overlooking the harbour. There, under leafy chestnut trees, at a sidewalk table shaded by an umbrella advertising Tourtel beer, Madame Béziers will draw up three chairs—one for herself, one for Renée and one for Racine. If she's expecting company, she might draw up a fourth or fifth one. Then, from a mustachioed waiter in a white tunic with gold buttons, she orders iced Dubonnet for herself and dishes of strawberry sorbet for Renée and Racine.

Though it is not uncommon to see dogs at the Café Gasconne, especially white poodles on a Sunday afternoon, they usually sit on the ground. Not so Renée. She sits on a chair and laps up her sorbet like a proper lady. Though she obviously savours it, she would never think of slurping or making a lot of noise.

It is less common, though by no means rare, to see a pussycat among the café society along rue Talmont. Unlike the poodles, they mostly sit on chairs. I've seen cats accompanied by people, and cats by themselves, but until I saw Renée and Racine, I'd never seen a cat accompanied by a dog. And yet, no one, not even the mustachioed waiter, deftly carrying his tray of drinks, seemed surprised. I believe the French are like that, especially in the south. They are not easily beguiled. They take animals at sidewalk cafés for granted. What could be more natural? There is lively conversation, tasty libation, so why deprive your pet of this social enjoyment? Life is short. Who knows what tomorrow may bring? Another iced vermouth, s'il vous plaît, garçon. And refills of sorbet for my friends.

I spent several pleasant Sunday afternoons with Madame Béziers at the Café Gasconne last summer. It always amused me to see her drive up in her little Deux

Chevaux, with the top down and her dog and cat in the back seat. She would carry them over to the table, place them on their chairs, and kiss me on both cheeks. Then she would remove her cap and gloves and sunglasses, and pull her chair close to mine. It was not difficult for me to imagine her as a happy young girl sixty years ago, riding around in her father's car, visiting the farms and vineyards of Poitou-Charentes. On more than one occasion, comparing her childhood to mine, I told her how lucky she'd been, how lucky she was to have such pleasant memories.

Meanwhile, Renée and Racine would sit sedately, looking around to see who was there. They could have been Hemingway and Fitzgerald at the Deux Magots in Paris, or Gertrude Stein and Alice B. Toklas, or Somerset Maugham and Graham Greene, or Oscar Wilde and Noel Coward. But they weren't. They were Renée and Racine, at the Café Gasconne, in La Rochelle.

One such Sunday, on the eve of my departure for Spain, I noticed that though the waiter had set down fresh saucers of sorbet, Racine the cat had not started his. It was as though he didn't realize it was there. He appeared lost in thought, staring blankly off into space, as, I must admit, he often did. It was obvious to me that the poodle, Renée, who by then had finished her second helping and licked the saucer clean, was thinking seriously about polishing off Racine's sorbet too. She even went so far as to sample it with her tongue. She seemed to be saying, "If you're not going to finish this, Brindle Cat, do you mind if I do?"

But then, to my astonishment, she pushed the saucer closer to Racine with her nose and gave him a little nudge on the shoulder. The cat then appeared to sniff about, which hardly seemed necessary, the sorbet being so close, and when he'd located it he began lapping it with gusto. His pink tongue fairly flew, his ears swiveled like antennae.

Puzzled, I looked closely at Racine's eyes, and for the first time noticed how opaque they were. "Madame Béziers," I said, "did you see that?"

"Did I see what, chéri?"

"Did you see your dog push the cat's saucer of sorbet over to him."

"Oh, she does that all the time. The eyesight of my poor Racine is not what it once was. Sometimes I think he doesn't see much at all anymore. I took him once to the Vet, but sadly there is no cure. I think my father could have done something."

"But that's remarkable."

"What is, mon petit chou?"

"That Renée wouldn't just eat the sorbet herself. I'm amazed."

"You mean you didn't know my cat was blind?"

"I had no idea."

"That proves how good he is at hiding it. Since a long time, I didn't know either. But then one day I see him walk into a wall and fall down a flight of stairs. Ever since then, the poodle looks out for him. I think maybe I should call Renée the Seeing Eye poodle. But you know what I think, mon cher? I think the cat hears better. I think poor Renée, she's almost deaf. If you call her when she sleeps, sometimes she doesn't answer. So between the two of them, they manage."

The afternoon was wearing on. Sailboats were scurrying in off the Bay of Biscay ahead of thunder clouds. At the cafés along rue Talmont, people were finishing their drinks, paying their tabs. Another Sunday afternoon was drawing to a close. My train to Biarritz was due in half an hour.

I must say, I felt sad at having to leave La Rochelle and Madame Béziers. Concerning her brindle cat's vision problems and her poodle's deafness, I'm not sure what I felt, but I don't think it was sadness.

I watched Madame Béziers carry Renée and Racine over to her car and place them in the back seat. I heard her ask them if they wanted the top up in case it rained. Evidently they said no, because a moment later she drove away with it still down. At the corner of rue Talmont, waiting for the traffic light, she waved farewell. Moments later, from beyond the sea wall, came an ominous rumble of thunder. Heading for the train station with my umbrella up, I stopped and looked back along the quay to the two ancient stone towers guarding the harbour entrance. Then the first raindrops fell and I had to hurry.

Chapter Sixteen

Have Cat, Will Travel

Bibesco (Bib, for short) is a small, grey, tiger-striped shorthair with turquoise eyes. She's eleven years old and belongs to Desmond Bryce, a professional cook. Their story is unusual because they've been all over North America together and have had some extraordinary experiences.

Fresh from the Food Services programme at Confederation College, Desmond Bryce began his cooking career at the Fort William Country Club. From there he moved to Rattler's, then to Papa Joe's, then to the Travelodge Motel, and finally to the Venture Inn. It was here he met his future ex-wife, Sheila. They were married that summer, honeymooned at Banff, and declared war shortly thereafter. According to Desmond, it was a marriage made in hell, whose main ingredient was mutual hostility. In the heat of battle, he had trouble remembering what he'd ever seen in Sheila and why they'd ever got married. The only thing they agreed on was that it had been a huge mistake. Insults and accusations flew. The end came one Sunday afternoon when Desmond experienced severe chest pains. He was sure he was having a heart attack. He said he remembered collapsing into a chair and begging Sheila to phone for an ambulance. Instead, she put on her hat and coat and went to a movie at Silver City. The last thing she said going out the door was that she was sick and tired of his histrionics, his hypochondria, his constant need to make her feel guilty.

This may be hard to believe, but no sooner had Sheila left than Desmond began to feel better. The pain subsided. He guessed he wasn't having a heart attack after all. His temporary discomfort had probably been caused by too much garlic in the Caesar salad. Still, it had been a scary occurrence and had revealed Sheila's total lack of concern for his welfare. Walking out on someone who might be having a heart attack demonstrated a callousness beyond measure.

Desmond and Sheila were divorced soon after, and Desmond said that maybe the fake heart attack had been a blessing in disguise. At least it had brought things to a head and shown the hopelessness of the situation. Since then, he and his ex-wife have not spoken. They've gone their separate ways and hope never to meet again.

Following his divorce, Desmond cooked briefly at the

Lakehead Psychiatric Hospital, at Old Fort William, and at the Prince Arthur Hotel, where he had a nice room on the third floor, overlooking the harbour. The trouble was, although he liked his work, and couldn't imagine doing anything else for a living, he was consumed by an irresistible restlessness, an urge to be in motion. He thought of becoming a railroad chef, but was not enamoured of trains. He almost answered an ad in a trade magazine for cooks on the Hibernia oil rig, until he remembered that such platforms are stationary, anchored to the sea floor. What he wished, he said, was that he'd lived back in the days of exploration, when cooks were needed to go on expeditions to the ends of the earth.

Ironically, it was at this inopportune juncture in his life that he acquired Bibesco, the little tiger-striped cat. Not that he'd meant to. Though always fond of cats, he had no desire to own one, to be tied down by one, especially when he was champing at the bit to travel.

What happened was, one of the waitresses at the Prince Arthur, a girl named Sibyl, asked Desmond if he'd baby-sit her cat while she went away for the weekend. What she didn't tell him was that she'd landed both a boyfriend and a new job in Vancouver and had no intention of returning. This he found out on Tuesday, when he got a letter from her, with no return address, in which she apologized, but said she didn't know what else to do. Although she adored the cat, she knew she couldn't take it with her. She'd been heart-broken, she said, to have to leave it. She said she hoped Desmond would forgive her, and that he'd take good care of little Bibesco. "She's clean, quiet and gentle," Sibyl wrote "If you're kind to her, and keep her litter box tidy, she'll give you no trouble."

And so there was Desmond, living in a hotel room, stuck with a cat when he least wanted one. He didn't even know why she was called Bibesco, unless it was because she had a small patch of white under her chin that looked like a bib. Thank God, just as Sibyl had said, she was a clean, quiet cat. She ate little, didn't seem fussy. Nor did she demand a lot of attention. She was affectionate without being obsessive, spent most of her time sleeping, and didn't resent being left alone. She was content to sit for hours looking out a window, yet was happy to see you come in the door, especially if you had a sliver of roast beef for her, or a nice bit of meatloaf. And if truth be told, Desmond liked her. They got along well. She slept on his bed at night, would sometimes lie behind his pillow and purr into his ear. And when he came up from the kitchen after putting in eight or ten hours preparing meals for finicky hotel guests, it was comforting to find her waiting, to have someone to talk to who didn't nag or argue.

That year, as navigation got into full swing and ships again entered the harbour from distant ports, Desmond's wanderlust became unbearable. On his days off, he sometimes went up to Hillcrest Park to watch the ships, or down to Keefer Terminal to see them unload. Sometimes he walked along the waterfront and watched grain boats taking on cargo at the elevators. Had it not been for Bibesco, he might very well have gone aboard the *Oakglen,* or the *Paterson*, or the *J.N. McWatters*, or the *Ralph Misener* and asked if they needed an experienced cook in the galley.

As it happened, he didn't need to do that, because one evening the chief engineer from the *Algomarine,* an old salt named Shepperton, came into the Prince Arthur

Hotel dining room, and after enjoying a succulent rack of lamb asked to send his compliments to the chef. So Desmond came out of the kitchen, wearing his white hat and apron, and shook the chief engineer's hand.

"Have you ever cooked aboard ship?" Shepperton asked him.

"No," Desmond said, "but I'd like to."

"The reason I ask, not that I'd ever try to lure you away from this hotel, is that we've just lost our chief cook on the *Algomarine* and I dread the thought of sailing without someone good in the galley. I can tell you, the wages are excellent, if you ever take a notion."

"But I'm not a member of the seafarers' union."

"Well, we could soon fix that."

"I'd have to give notice here, of course."

"You mean to say you'd seriously consider sailing with us? I was really only joking. But if I thought you could be persuaded, I'd speak to the captain. We'll be back up here in ten days."

"There's only one small problem."

"Your wife would throw a tantrum?"

"I don't have a wife. What I have is a cat."

"A cat? Well, that's no problem. The first mate has his Pomeranian pup on board. And I've sailed with cats before. Lots of them. I once crossed the Atlantic with a radio officer who had two cats. They had the run of the ship. So if that's all that's stopping you, don't give it another thought."

"I could bring my cat along?"

"Absolutely. As long as it's neutered, housebroken and vaccinated, there's nothing in the regulations to prevent it. Shall I speak to the captain?"

"You say you'll be back in ten days?"

"Maybe eleven."

"Then yes, I wish you would."

"You're serious?"

"I'm serious. Never more so."

"In that case, chef Bryce, I'm glad I came to the Prince Arthur for dinner tonight."

Desmond shook the chief engineer's hand, gave him his phone number. "So am I," he said. "You have no idea. All I have to do now is inform Bib that she's about to become a ship's cat."

"I once sailed with a parrot," Shepperton said. "It only knew a dozen words, none of them fit for mixed company."

Desmond and Bibesco sailed on the Algoma Central's self-unloader *Algomarine* the rest of that season, and the next, and the next. Mainly they voyaged between Thunder Bay and Montreal, with side trips to Cleveland and Detroit. Once they delivered a load of limestone to Toledo. Another time they took a million bushels of corn from Chicago to Duluth, and on the return trip carried iron ore to Erie, Pennsylvania. A week later, they filled their holds with potash destined for Sorel, Quebec.

Bibesco's adaptation to life on the high seas was instantaneous. She seemed to understand the purpose of ships. According to Desmond, it was not unusual to see her up in the wheelhouse, lying in the sun on the chart table, helping negotiate the flight locks of the Welland Canal. Fortunately, the first mate took a shine to her, patiently explained the uses of radar and GPS navigation. Members of the deck crew warned her to be careful going up and down companionways in rough weather. Two places she was not allowed were the galley and the engine room. Not that she would have been tempted to visit the latter anyway, with its heat and noise and steep ladders. She had her litter box in the paint locker and took most of her meals in Desmond's cabin, except for those special occasions when she was invited into the officers' dining room and given a dish of gravy on the floor. The chief steward, an older man named Peabody, from Yarmouth, Nova Scotia, was forever finding her asleep and sketching her in charcoal. It was his theory that cats are so calm aboard ships because they enjoy the feel of the engines' vibrations through their paws.

But cruising the Great Lakes and the St. Lawrence Seaway on the *Algomarine* was never the total extent of Bibesco's travels in any given year. In the off-season, she and Desmond went by car to Victoria, Seattle, San Diego and Galveston. One winter, they even spent a few days in Vancouver looking for Sibyl, but were unable to find her.

And if Bibesco liked shipboard life, she liked car travel even more. She would sit either in the rear window, or on Desmond's left shoulder, with one foot braced against the door, and watch the passing scene. She saw the cornfields of Kansas, the apple orchards of Iowa, the dairy farms of Nebraska. She was wide-eyed going through the Badlands of South Dakota, agape crossing the endless prairie of Wyoming, where she saw no deer or antelope but a few buffalo and vast herds of beef cattle. She was awestruck by the beauty of Idaho and the Blue Mountains of Oregon. In California, she would have been hard pressed to choose between the splendour of the Sierra Nevada and the panoramic seascapes along the coast highway. She was, in Desmond's view, "born to boogie."

At night, they stopped at inexpensive motels that did not exclude cats. Sometimes, when Desmond asked, desk clerks told him he could stay but Bibesco couldn't, and he would drive on and look for someplace else, rather than leave her in the car. Eventually he learned not to ask. He would carry Bibesco in under his jacket, open her a tin of cat food, and place her litter box in the closet. If it had been a long day's drive, she would often fall asleep watching television. In the morning they would consult the road map and get an early start. Once, on the outskirts of Amarillo, when Desmond stopped at a Perkins restaurant for breakfast, the waitress serving him looked out the window and saw Bibesco alone in the car, and because she loved cats insisted he go and bring her in. Which he did, and Bib sat beside him in the booth and had a feed of ham and eggs. The waitress made a fuss over her, stroked her fur, said how pretty she was, and when Desmond explained that the two of them spent their summers on Great Lakes freighters, the waitress shook her head in wonder. "I've never heard of a nautical cat," she said, and as they were leaving, gave Desmond a slice of ham and some bacon for Bibesco's lunch.

In Galveston, they drove down to the docks and saw the steamer *Stella Solaris* boarding passengers for a cruise to South America. Desmond parked the car and they sat and watched, and were still there when the ship's lines were cast off and she sailed out into Galveston Bay. "What would you think, Old Girl," Desmond asked Bib, "about working on a saltie?"

Though Bibesco was noncommittal, when Desmond got home to Thunder Bay he wrote a letter to Royal Olympic Cruises in Piraeus, owners of the *Stella Solaris*, and asked if they needed a seagoing, English-speaking chef. Or rather, a seagoing, English-speaking chef with a cat. A month later, he received a very nice letter, on embossed stationery, from the director of personnel for Royal Olympic, telling him that if he were a paid-up member of the International Seafarers' Union and in possession of his master chef's papers, and if he wished to sign a nine-month contract, they'd send him an application form. Unfortunately, however, he must realize that he would not be permitted to bring any live pets with him, as countries visited by the ship had stringent health and Customs formalities. And so Desmond gave up the idea of working for Royal Olympic Cruise Lines. As he told Bibesco, he wasn't all that keen on going to South America anyway. Greece, maybe, but not Patagonia.

The next season, Desmond and Bibesco sailed aboard the self-unloader *Algowood*, carrying iron ore pellets from Marquette to Sault Ste. Marie. The season after that they went aboard the smaller *Baie St. Paul*, and from then until the present time have been on the bulk freighter *Canadian Ranger*, hauling grain from Thunder Bay to Montreal.

It was on *Canadian Ranger*, the summer before last, that Bibesco committed what could be considered her most serious faux pas as a sailor. Had the truth ever got out, this incident might very well have ended her maritime career.

It all started one morning when the captain of the *Ranger*, a Greek named Philipopolis, happened to notice a small pigeon on deck, just aft of the starboard lifeboat. The ship was crossing Lake Erie at the time, downbound, and Captain Philipopolis assumed the bird was from Detroit. It was not uncommon for birds to hitch rides on grain boats, especially pigeons. Sometimes they stayed a few hours, sometimes a few days, sometimes they rode all the way to Montreal. The captain's favourite birds were the little nuthatches, who often boarded with the pilot in the middle of Lake St.

Clair and went up and down the rigging feasting on winged insects. Pigeons, on the other hand, were more apt to take shelter under the lifeboats or behind the ventilators, where they could find protection from the wind. Captain Philipopolis liked to put out bread-crumbs for them, and soda crackers, and even bowls of water. He said he admired the courage of land birds so far from shore. On this particular voyage, in the middle of Lake Erie, it was his opinion that the pigeon on deck was a homing pigeon, or possibly a racing pigeon, because it had a band on its leg. He said that if it was in a race, he didn't expect it to stay very long before taking flight again. At lunch he revealed that as a boy in Athens he had raised pigeons and had great respect for them. Before going to his cabin for an afternoon nap, he put out a handful of raisins.

Later in the afternoon, because it was warm and sunny after two days of rain, Desmond stepped out on deck for a breath of fresh air. Though he seldom took Bibesco with him, on this occasion, since she was there and seemed interested, he allowed her to accompany him.

Unfortunately, the pigeon was at that precise moment sleeping in the sun beside the lifeboat. Because Desmond had never seen Bibesco stalk anything, much less catch anything, he failed to perceive danger. Indeed, ever since he'd known her, Bib had been an indoor cat. He'd always assumed that her hunting instincts, if she'd had any, were dead. As he was soon to discover, they were only dormant.

He watched, fascinated, as she crouched, stretched out her neck, lashed her tail back and forth, and began slithering along the deck toward the sleeping, unsus-pecting pigeon. Even then, Des thought her purpose would simply be to sneak up on the bird and scare it.

He was flabbergasted, he said, when Bib suddenly leapt through the air, caught the pigeon in her claws, and before he could even think of reacting, had crunched its iridescent neck in her jaws and killed it. He said she looked quite proud of herself, even carried the pigeon around for a few moments, while it quivered in death. Then, surprisingly, shockingly, she began pulling its feathers off with her teeth, as though trying to get at its soft underbelly.

And that's when Desmond knew he had to do something, when he realized that Bib meant to eat the pigeon. Fortunately, there was no one else on deck. No one had seen this dastardly deed. Though impressed with Bib's skill and cunning, Desmond understood he must quickly dispose of the evidence before Captain Philipopolis got up from his nap and came looking for the bird. And so, breaking the rule about not throwing things overboard, he took the corpse from between Bib's teeth and tossed it over the side. He said Bib gave him a look of disbelief, tinged with anger, as though asking, "How would you like it if I deep-sixed your grilled cheese sandwich?" Furtively, he picked up the telltale feathers. Then he put Bib under his arm and hurried to his cabin with her. There he left her, and proceeded to the galley to start supper.

That evening, when Captain Philipopolis asked if anyone knew the whereabouts of his pigeon, no one said anything, because no one knew. "I guess," he said, "it flew away, anxious to continue its journey and get home. Just like me."

In Montreal last summer, Desmond met Aquinus Baarshers, chief cook on the *Cast Otter*, an ocean-going container ship on its way to Belgium. "If you ever tire of inland sailing," Aquinus told Desmond, "which is like sailing on a pond, you should consider coming to work for me on the *Cast Otter*. I think you would enjoy it. Life is very unhurried crossing the Atlantic, at least in summer. It takes twelve days each way, and so you have time to relax and be a philosopher as well as a chef. I would be happy to show you Zeebrugge, Antwerp, Brussels. I could put in a good word for you with the captain."

"Would I be able to bring my cat?"

"I don't see why not. The quartermaster has a canary."

"In that case, I'll think about it. But I make no promise."

"I myself will leave the *Cast Otter* at the end of my present contract and go aboard the *Princesse de Provence*, a gourmet riverboat which cruises down the Rhône from Lyon to Avignon, carrying wealthy European passengers. Do you speak French?"

"A little," Desmond said.

"Then why don't you join me? As it happens, I shall be in need of a sous-chef."

"It sounds very enticing, very interesting. I just might. Would I be able to bring my cat?"

"That I'm not sure of. We would have to ask."

Which is pretty much how things stand in Desmond's life at the moment. He says there's a good chance his next ship will be the *Cast Otter*. And after that, who knows? Maybe the gourmet river boat, *Princesse de Provence*. He says he's always wanted to see the south of France, and this might be a way of doing it. Of course, if he crosses the Atlantic and is gone for nine or ten months, it will mean packing an extra suitcase. As far as easygoing, adaptable Bibesco is concerned, it shouldn't matter much, because she travels light anyway.

Chapter Seventeen

Ginger, Caught in the Act

M̲r. Cornelius, who owned a downtown apartment building, was considered by some to be
a heartless landlord. He may very well have been. One
of his rules was: no pets. So a few years ago, when he
evicted a single mother and her two children because

they could no longer afford the rent, he was both surprised and annoyed to find they'd left behind a calico cat named Ginger. He was surprised because he didn't know about the cat, and annoyed for the same reason. As he often said, he was running a tenement, not an animal shelter. Exactly what his reasons were for not allowing pets, no one knew, but after this particular eviction, he went around and checked all the other apartments for animals.

At about this time, his sister Agnes, a widow well past middle age, who lived across town in a bungalow near Boulevard Lake and whose children had all moved to distant cities, decided that what she needed to combat loneliness was a dog. Or a cat. Or a parrot. Or a goldfish. Some other living creature to share her house and be dependent on her.

So when her brother happened to mention the calico cat that was wandering around the apartment building downtown, wondering where its previous owners had gone, Agnes said she'd take it if nobody else would.

"But why would you want a cat, Agnes?" Mr. Cornelius asked her. "Cats are a nuisance, always under foot. You can't take a cat for a walk or make it retrieve sticks."

"I wouldn't want to," Agnes said. "As long as it's neutered and housebroken and mature enough to appreciate peace and quiet. Unlike you, brother, I've always liked cats. At the moment I need something to share my empty nest."

"I could rent you one of my apartments."

"No, thank you. I prefer my house. It may be empty, but it's full of memories. What kind of cat is it?"

"I believe it's what's called a tortoise shell. It's not a Persian, and it's not a Siamese, so I think it must be a tortoise shell."

"What colour is it?"

"It's several colours. Grey, yellow, black, orange."

"Does it have white on it?"

"Yes, quite a bit of white."

"Then it's a calico, not a tortoise shell. Tortoise shells don't have white. What's its name?"

Mr. Cornelius snorted, made other derogatory noises. "How the hell should I know? It's a cat, for God's sake, not a person."

So that's how Agnes ended up with Ginger, the calico cat, who, though neutered and housebroken and possessed of a pleasant disposition, had no interest whatsoever in going for walks or retrieving sticks. The first thing Agnes did was give Ginger title to a small bedroom at the back of the house, one that had been used by her youngest son before he went off and joined the army. She put a nice bedspread on the cot, added a few tasteful cushions, stuck up pictures of cats taken from last year's calendar. Ginger seemed to understand right off the bat that this was to be her room, and when she wasn't sprawled on the living room floor or looking out the kitchen window, she spent a lot of time there. It's where her litter box was. It's where she went when she wanted a little privacy, and to take her daily bath.

Another thing Agnes did was test Ginger to see what kind of cat food she preferred. She went to the A & P and got a bag of assorted tins and packets, from which she was able to determine that Ginger's favourite was Whiskas chicken. Though her ribs showed when she first moved in, and her fur lacked lustre, it wasn't long before she was as beautiful as any of the pedigree cats in the calendar pictures.

There was only one glitch in this otherwise near-perfect arrangement. Quite early on, Agnes could tell that Ginger wanted to spend time outdoors. First thing in the morning and last thing at night, and several times during the day, she would sit at the door and meow vociferously. It didn't take a rocket scientist to know what she wanted. Agnes debated getting a leash for her and walking her like a dog. But she didn't. She thought about tying her to the end of a rope and letting her out in the back yard. But she didn't do that either. Subscribing to the belief that a cat should be free to come and go as it pleases, she went to Beaver Lumber and bought an eight-foot two-by-four, to which she nailed slats, and propped this makeshift ladder against the wall at the back of the house, under Ginger's bedroom window. "There," she said. "I know you're a sensible cat, and a grateful cat, and you won't leave the back yard. You have everything you need right here: trees, grass, flowers, an old stone wall, an iron gate to keep bothersome dogs and children out."

When her brother, Mr. Cornelius, the landlord, phoned and asked how things were going, she told him they couldn't be better. Adaptable Ginger was good company, and now that she had her own means of ingress and egress, caused no trouble at all. She said she could tell that Ginger was perfectly content and felt right at home, because she purred a lot. Like Agnes, she enjoyed tranquillity. There were no noisy children to disturb her, no dogs to contend with. Indeed, she lived in cat utopia, with a room to herself, daily combings, the finest cuisine. And best of all, she could go out her window anytime she felt like it, could go for a stroll in the garden, and come back in when the spirit moved her. Agnes was pleased to see her basking in the sun on the garden wall with her eyes closed, as though meditating. When ladies came over for afternoon tea and a game of whist, sociable Ginger would put in an appearance, would parade through with her tail aloft, and allow everyone to praise and touch her. "What a lovely cat, Agnes," people would exclaim. "How lucky you are. She's obviously devoted to you."

"As well she should be," Agnes said on more than one occasion. "I rescued her from that awful tenement of my brother's. I gave her dignity and a quiet place to live."

And so Agnes was perplexed one day a few weeks later when Mrs. Bloomquist, her card partner and neighbour from six doors down, at the far end of the crescent, offhandedly remarked how much she enjoyed Ginger's visits.

"You mean her visits to our little tea parties?" Agnes said.

"No," said Mrs. Bloomquist, "I mean her visits to my house."

Agnes thought this over. "You must be seeing things, Mrs. Bloomquist. Ginger never leaves my backyard, so she couldn't very well visit you."

"Well, but I think she does, my dear. She meows at my door and I let her in. She often accepts a tidbit, or helps herself to the dog's dinner."

"Well, then, for certain it can't be Ginger. Ginger is very fussy about what she eats, and under no circumstances would she go anywhere near a dog. She's afraid of dogs. Detests them. No, my dear Mrs. Bloomquist, I'm quite sure you're mistaken. It must be another cat. It couldn't be my Ginger."

Mrs. Bloomquist persisted. "It looks like your cat, Agnes. It has exactly the same colours, the same jade green eyes. And it seems to know me."

"But I tell you, it can't be. Ginger never leaves home. And you say you have a dog?"

"Yes. Old Basil, our basset hound. He's harmless. He snarls a bit at strangers, but as far as we know, he's never bitten anyone."

"And what time of day does this look-alike cat visit you?"

"Oh, anytime. In the morning. In the afternoon. Last thing at night, before the children go to bed. It comes in and says hello to everyone, has a bite to eat, sits on the couch with Tess and Tyler, my twins."

"I'll tell you what, Mrs. Bloomquist. Next time this imposter visits you, call me on the phone. I'll make sure Ginger is here, and we'll put this mystery to rest."

After that, though she remained skeptical, Agnes took more notice of Ginger's comings and goings. She checked on her whereabouts a dozen times a day, followed her about the garden, looked in on her during the night. She even bought her a fluorescent pink flea collar that glowed in the dark.

And then one day, having spent the afternoon downtown shopping, she received a phone call from Mrs. Bloomquist. "Your cat is here now, Agnes," Mrs. Bloomquist said. "She walked in an hour ago."

"Is she wearing a flea collar?" Agnes asked.

"Yes, as a matter of fact, she is. A fluorescent pink one."

So Agnes hurried into Ginger's room, and of course it was empty. She went out into the garden—also empty. She looked through all the other rooms in the house—no cat. And so she put on her coat and walked briskly round the crescent to Mrs. Bloomquist's house.

She marched up Mrs. Bloomquist's stairs, was ushered into the living room, and there, sure enough, sitting on the sofa as smug as you please, was Ginger. No doubt about it. Fluorescent pink flea collar and all. Basil the basset hound sat on a nearby chair, his tongue hanging out, grumbling softly to himself. Mrs. Bloomquist's twins, Tess and Tyler, were brushing Ginger, calling her Fluffy, decorating her with ribbons, asking their mother why they couldn't have a cat. The T.V. was on, the stereo was playing. Down in the basement, Mr. Bloomquist was cutting lumber with his power saw. Bombarded with all these sounds, Agnes had the impression of barely subdued mayhem.

What puzzled her, of course, was Ginger's apparent composure. That is, until the cat rolled over and perceived her scowling mistress, and then Agnes was rewarded with a look of surprise, not to say astonishment, tinged, unless she was mistaken, with a modicum of guilt.

"Ginger?" she said, levelling an accusatory finger, as an irate wife might do, upon discovering her husband in a speakeasy with his arm around the barmaid. "Ginger, you naughty cat. And to think I went out of my way and incurred expense to provide you with privacy."

It was an awkward situation, as she told her brother, Mr. Cornelius, next day. The Bloomquist children, setting up a clamour, were all for keeping Fluffy, or Ginger, if Agnes had been willing to part with her, which she wasn't. In the midst of their pleadings, having perhaps reached the end of his tether, Basil the basset hound chose that moment to begin braying at the top of his voice. He may have been overcome with jealousy, and if so, who could blame him? After all, nobody was tying ribbons on him, and he might look good in ribbons. And why didn't he possess a stylish pink collar like this indolent feline trespasser who had the gall to help herself to his food? Hearing the commotion, Mr. Bloomquist came clumping up from the basement, demanding an explanation. "What the hell's going on here?" he wanted to know.

Being an astute cat, and sensing that she was on the point of wearing out her welcome, Ginger extricated herself from the twins, Tess and Tyler. Turning a deaf ear toward Basil, she jumped nimbly to the floor. "I'm outa here," she may have said, or at least thought. It seemed a propitious moment to pick her up, and so Agnes did. "Would it be better, do you think," she asked, "if I took my cat home now?"

"It might be," Mrs. Bloomquist said. "But we'd be happy to see you both again, whenever you feel like visiting. Our door is always open to our friends."

"Thank you," Agnes said, hurrying down the stairs with Ginger in her arms, heading for home at a brisk pace. "Fluffy, indeed!" she could be heard muttering.

As she told her brother, Mr. Cornelius, a day or two later, she was of two minds about giving the cat back to him. "I don't demand much," she said. "But I do demand loyalty, and my cat has been very disloyal."

"I don't agree with you, Agnes," Mr. Cornelius said. "She's not been disloyal, only friendly. She's what you'd call gregarious. It's no crime to spread yourself around and cheer people up."

"But she snuck out of the house while my back was turned."

"She knew how you felt and was only trying to spare your feelings. She missed being with kids. Who else would tie ribbons on her? I'd say, give her another chance. Take away the ladder, if you must. Close the window. But please, whatever you do, Agnes, don't bring her back here."

And Agnes didn't. When she'd had time to think it over, she realized that her brother, for all his faults, was probably right—cats, being hedonists, have no conception of disloyalty. And really, there was enough of Ginger to go around. So she left the window open and the ladder up, and Ginger was free to come and go as she pleased. Strangely though, she seemed less interested in going places alone after that. Oh, she still spent time in the garden, still sat on the old stone wall with her eyes closed and the sun on her fur, as though meditating. But when leaves fell and cold weather came, she hardly went out at all.

Chapter Eighteen

Stan & Suzy

Norton took to outdoor life immediately.
It was a little frightening how easy it was
to begin thinking of him as a country squire.
    -Peter Gethers: *The Cat Who Went to Paris*

I do not wish to give the impression that
Polar Bear was, in his latter years, more
difficult than when he was younger. In
many ways, he was less difficult."
    -Cleveland Amory: *The Best Cat Ever*

A year into their marriage, Faith and Julian Denison acquired two white kittens from the custodian at Julian's school, Port Arthur Collegiate. Though the cats were brother and sister, their personalities were as different as night and day. From the outset, Stan was a timid, shy creature, always wanting to hide behind something, to have someone else go first and make sure it was safe. His sister Suzy, on the other hand, was reckless, bold as brass, impulsive. She was an impatient cat. While her brother was content with routine, she was always on the lookout for something new—a new game, a new food, a new place to sleep.

Curiously, for the first few years, their names weren't Stan and Suzy. The day Julian brought them home, he introduced them to Faith as Tristan and Isolde. When she asked him why, he told her about King Mark of Cornwall sending his young nephew, Tristan, to Ireland to fetch back a promised bride, the beautiful Isolde. According to Arthurian legend, however, during the return trip, Tristan and Isolde became ardent lovers, and when jealous King Mark found out, he had them both beheaded.

"Those are strange names for cats," Faith suggested. "I'm not sure they'll stick."

"Sure they will," Julian said. "I really like that story, and so do my students. Tristan and Isolde. Perfect monikers for two spotless white cats."

Which they might very well have been, except that none of the Denison children (there were eventually three: Britney, Elspeth and Barry) could pronounce the cats' names. Not that they didn't try. As soon as they could talk, each of them made an attempt at Tristan and Isolde. In Britney's case, what came out sounded more like Kiss and Sooly. Which Elspeth later refined to

Tam and Shirley. And finally little Barry, a forceful child, corrected everyone by insisting the cats be called Stan and Suzy.

"No, children," Julian would protest. "Their names are Tristan and Isolde. Can everyone say that? Tristan and Isolde."

"Stan and Suzy!" the children would shout. "Stan and Suzy!"

Which always brought both cats running, because if they recognized any words at all, which is fairly questionable, it was Stan and Suzy.

Eventually Julian gave up insisting they be called Tristan and Isolde, even though he still liked that story and continued teaching it to his senior students.

"It's a good thing," Faith pointed out, by way of consolation, "that you didn't name them Troilus and Cressida, or Héloïse and Abelard. I hate to think what the kids would be calling them."

In the meantime, Stan and Suzy (or Tristan and Isolde, which is what Julian called them when the children weren't around) grew into fine, good-looking cats. Though Stan retained his basic timidity, he would, when in the mood, wrestle with his sister, chase her up and down the cellar stairs, hide in the den and pounce on her when she came searching. The thing was, Suzy would often have to instigate these games. She was clever at provoking Stan, rousing him from sleep with a casual nip on the tail, convincing him that what she needed was a dose of discipline. Had she wanted to, she could easily have outrun him or headed him off at the pass. As it was, she often spooked him, scared him out of his wits by lying in ambush at the kitchen door, or exploding from the clothes hamper on laundry day.

When they wrestled and the fur flew, Suzy could, by superior strength and cunning, always get the better of Stan. When she'd had enough, she would pin him, flip him on his back, give him two or three good swats and walk away disdainfully, another victory to her credit.

To look at them, you wouldn't have thought Stan and Suzy cared much for each other. Perhaps they didn't. Or perhaps they just didn't show it. They could go days without communicating. They ate at different times, slept in different rooms. Like two ships passing in the night, they could walk by each other without acknowledgment, without recognition. On warm summer days, the children sometimes took them out on leashes into the back yard, where they would roll on the grass and sniff flowers. It was obvious that Suzy enjoyed this activity. She would crouch and pursue butterflies, prick up her ears at sounds from neighbouring yards: dogs barking, birds singing, parents fighting. On one occasion, Rascal, the arthritic, nearly blind Airedale from next door, came wandering through the hedge, and though Suzy crouched and took a defensive stance, Stan bolted for the house. He got up such a head of steam that he jerked the leash right out of Elspeth's hand. When she caught up with him, he was cowering at the back door, eyes wide with fright. "That's only blind old Rascal," Elspeth told him, but all Stan wanted to do was go indoors and hide.

Sadly, after ten years of marriage, during which time they'd had their share of spats and differences, Julian and Faith Denison went their separate ways. Part of the problem stemmed from Faith's desire to resume her career as a dental hygienist. Julian didn't want her to. He wanted her to stay home and look after the children, even though by then all three were in school. The other thing he didn't like about her working full time was that in the evenings and on weekends she expected him to do housework. He also disapproved of her proximity to the suave, handsome dentist she worked for, Dr. Bucknell, a divorced ex-boyfriend of hers. This despite the fact that Julian himself was paying heavy attention to a vivacious colleague at Port Arthur Collegiate, a Miss Voorhees, who taught French and theatre arts. They sat together in the lunch room, did hall duty together, stopped off at the Brew Pub for drinks after school. At the staff picnic in June, the two of them disappeared into the woods for an hour, missing the frisbee-throwing contest. At the golf tournament a week later, they did the same thing, and if people hadn't been talking before, they were now, because on the way home, after wetting their whistles at Rattler's, they'd been involved in a traffic accident on Red River Road. As though that weren't bad enough, next day their pictures were on the front page of the newspaper.

And so by mutual consent, after one particularly horrendous weekend of squabbling and name-calling, during which time the children had hidden in their bedrooms, crying, and the cats had taken refuge in the cellar, Julian packed two suitcases and moved to the Landmark Hotel. He stayed there ten days, then became a permanent guest at Miss Voorhees' apartment. Meanwhile, Faith hired a housekeeper recommended to her by Dr. Bucknell, an Irish lady named Mrs. de Valera, from county Armagh, and things more or less settled down.

Not that everyone was happy. The Denison children definitely were not. They didn't like Dr. Bucknell all that much, even though he came for dinner almost every night and on Sunday afternoons gave them rides in his luxurious new Chrysler minivan. The trouble was, they missed their father and couldn't understand why he'd abandoned them. Of course he missed them too, and, as he would later admit, he missed Tristan and Isolde.

In the fall, not unexpectedly, divorce proceedings were started. While they were going on, Julian and Miss Voorhees moved into a two-bedroom duplex on Farrand Street. They would have been just as well off in her apartment, except that Julian's children would have been unable to stay overnight when it was his turn to have them.

Not long after, Dr. Bucknell sold his condominium on the fourteenth floor of Waverley Park Towers and moved in with Faith. It made sense. Why maintain multiple households when one would do? Though he found Britney, Elspeth and Barry tiresome at times, and on occasion asked them to make less noise and stop chattering, there was room for everyone. Few major adjustments were necessary. For the children, the only real difference was that a new Daddy was sleeping in Mommy's bed. And when they went to visit their father on Farrand Street, Miss Voohees stuffed them with pizza and ice cream.

Unfortunately, what the adults had overlooked in these arrangements was the absence of cats at Julian's house on Farrand Street. When Britney and Elspeth stayed there every second weekend, they were distressed beyond measure at having to leave Stan and Suzy with their mother. Julian would hear them crying in the spare bedroom, and when he went in to see what was the matter, the girls told him that despite the dolls Miss

Voorhees had bought them, despite the pizza and ice cream, they wanted to go home and see their cats.

"But that's ridiculous," Julian said. "Surely you can get along without Tristan and Isolde for a weekend. You'll see them on Monday. Tomorrow we'll go to the park. We'll go sailing on Boulevard Lake. We'll go feed the bears at Chippewa."

But that was of little comfort to Britney and Elspeth, who couldn't sleep without Stan snuggled between them and Suzy purring in their ears. They said they could picture their furry friends alone in the dark, meowing sadly.

Alternate weekends, when Barry came to stay, things were a tad better, because he was more fascinated with Miss Voorhees and less lonesome for the cats. He was also happy to be rid of his sisters, to be the sole object of his father's attention, to be allowed as many slices of pizza as he wished. But if truth be told, the first thing he did when he got home Sunday night was find Stan and Suzy and gather them up in his arms, letting them know he was back.

Not surprisingly, the day came when Britney and Elspeth told their mother they didn't wish to visit Julian anymore unless they could take the cats with them. Dr. Bucknell, who, let's be honest, relished their absence every second weekend, and who was, moreover, a dog lover, said, "Fine, take the damn cats to Farrand Street with you. Leave them there, if you want. But don't stop going."

As you might guess, when feisty young Barry got wind of this, he stood his ground, put his foot down, threatened a tantrum. The cats, he said, belonged at home, with him. It was what they were used to. If they went to Farrand Street, they would surely run away. At best, they'd be unhappy. Besides, he'd once heard Miss Voorhees say she didn't care for cats. In fact, she thought she might be rather allergic to them.

It was Dr. Bucknell, the clever dentist, who came up with what he thought was a brilliant solution. Why not, he suggested, have one cat living at each residence? That way, everyone would be content. Britney and Elspeth could install Suzy at Miss Voorhees' house on Farrand Street, while timid Stan stayed home with Barry. In his view, it sometimes required a decisive, clear-thinking outsider to solve a sticky family problem.

Julian said later he should have known this wouldn't work. Not with Tristan and Isolde. He said someone should have warned him, should have spoken up. The children, gifted with insight, realized from the start that it was a stupid idea, but, erroneously believing grownups to be infallible, kept silent.

One Friday evening, Britney and Elspeth put Suzy in a cat carrier and took her to Miss Voorhees' house on Farrand Street. They took along her litter box and a supply of her favourite cat food. They spent all day Saturday and half of Sunday trying to acclimatize her to her new surroundings. While Julian was happy enough to see her, Miss Voorhees was not. She was especially worried that during the week, when Suzy was home alone, she might shed white fur all over everything and make a general mess. Miss Voorhees, as Julian had by now discovered, tended to be overly fastidious. On the way home Sunday night, Britney and Elspeth sat in the back seat of Julian's car, weeping.

They hadn't realized how traumatic it would be, leaving Suzy behind in a strange house. True, she'd have Julian, and they'd have Stan, but still they cried.

Which is what timid Stan had been doing since Friday—crying piteously and looking upstairs and down for Suzy. He kept Faith and Dr. Bucknell awake all night, going from room to room, expressing his loneliness. Sunday night, and every night thereafter, Suzy cried too, looking through Miss Voorhees' house for Stan. Like him, she refused to eat. Nor would she use her litter box. Miss Voorhees was furious when she came home after a hard day teaching French and theatre arts and found her couch stained and her carpet soiled. When she scolded Suzy for these misdemeanours, Suzy responded with a hiss and a look of contempt.

Once established, living arrangements, no matter how unsatisfactory, are not easily renounced. Dr. Bucknell didn't want Suzy back. Neither did he want Britney and Elspeth at home every second weekend. There were times when he longed for the peaceful serenity of his fourteenth-floor condo in Waverley Park Towers. No cats, no kids, no turmoil. He may well have been asking himself whether life with Faith was worth it.

Meanwhile, Miss Voorhees was on the point of laying down an ultimatum. Either Suzy left, or she would. She was growing tired not only of the cat, whom Julian insisted on calling Isolde, but of Britney, Elspeth and Barry as well, all of whom, in her opinion, were at times noisy and disrespectful. The maddening part was that Julian, afraid of losing their affection, raised neither his hand nor his voice to any of them, even when they deserved it. As did that repulsive, reclusive, obnoxious cat, who refused to eat and meowed all night at the bedroom door. It was going to be a race, she said, to see if the cat died of starvation before she throttled it with her bare hands. On hearing this, Britney and Elspeth went into hysterics, while Julian began to suspect that somewhere along the line he might have made a mistake.

Faith would say later that it pained her to see timid Stan grow thinner and thinner from not eating. He stayed down in the basement, seldom coming upstairs, except to meander listlessly through the house, meowing forlornly. The Irish housekeeper, Mrs. de Valera, said she could put up with the meowing, but didn't want to be there when poor Stan died of malnutrition. "He's pining away over something, he is," she told Faith on more than one occasion. "There's something breaking his poor wee heart, and I hate to see it."

It was young Barry who announced to his mother one day that things could not go on like this. "Suzy has to come back here," he said.

"If she does," Faith pointed out, "your sisters won't go and stay with your father."

"Then he should come back here too."

Which gave Faith momentary pause. "I'm afraid that's not likely to happen, my child. Dr. Bucknell lives here now. Your father lives with Miss Voorhees. Soon, he and I will be divorced."

Barry clenched his small fists, made a terrible face, "I don't like Dr. Bucknell anymore. He's always telling me and Stan to be quiet. If he stays, I'm going to run away from home."

At that, Faith drew him to her, held him very close. Not because she thought he'd carry out his threat, but because she too had begun to tire of Dr. Bucknell. For one thing, he went out alone almost every evening and came home smelling of perfume. His ardour for her had cooled considerably. His intolerant criticism of her children had become a bone of contention.

And then one Sunday evening, there at Faith's door stood Julian. Britney and Elspeth were with him. So was Suzy. He said, "I've brought Isolde home. Things didn't work out. She wouldn't eat, wouldn't use her litter box. All she did was mope around and meow. The kids tell me Tristan's the same way. I guess it wasn't a good idea to split them up. So I brought her home."

"Look at her," Faith said. "She's nothing but skin and bones. And you, Julian. How are you?"

Julian hesitated perceptibly. "Fine," he said. "Never better."

"Will you come in for coffee? I'm alone this evening. We could talk about the divorce."

And so Julian did, and was there to witness the reunion of Stan and Suzy. He said later that it was an interesting experience. As soon as the two cats saw each other they both ran forward, chirped a greeting and eagerly touched noses. Suzy gave Stan a lusty lick on the head. Then she proceeded to ignore him. It was as though she hadn't missed him at all. She wandered through the house with Stan at her heels and all three children bringing up the rear. Faith said it looked like a parade, like a procession of pilgrims. All they needed was a drum. She put down two dishes of food and everyone stood back while the cats took the edge off their appetites. When the dishes were empty, Faith refilled them and again everyone stood back. Under different circumstances, Julian said, it would have been a demonstration of gluttony. Satiated and silent for the first time in weeks, Stan and Suzy then retired to the girls' bedroom, where they curled up on the blankets, put their tails over their noses, and fell asleep back to back. Which was something they hadn't done since they were kittens. From the doorway you could hear them purring like idling diesel engines on a frosty winter morning.

Later, sitting at the kitchen table drinking coffee with Faith, Julian admitted that things were not going well over on Farrand Street. Miss Voorhees, he said, had developed a cool negativity toward their relationship. She seemed less tolerant of his shortcomings, less willing to share him with the children. Not only that, at school she'd gone behind his back and switched her hall duty so as to be teamed up with Rocky, the new boys' Phys. Ed. teacher.

"By the way, dear." he said, "I haven't had a decent cup of coffee or a good night's sleep since I moved out."

Which is where the story of Stan and Suzy (or Tristan and Isolde) ends, I suppose. Except to say that the following day, according to Mrs. de Valera, the Irish housekeeper, the cats spent a lot of time wrestling on the living room floor, filling their stomachs, chasing each other up and down the cellar stairs. Stan, she said, had quit meowing and was less afraid of shadows. It seemed to her that he actually came close to winning a few of the wrestling matches.

Mrs. de Valera, an observant woman, became aware of certain other changes in the Denison household too. For one thing, the children, Britney, Elspeth and Barry, were much happier. Their long faces magically disappeared, when, at the end of the month, Dr. Bucknell moved back into Waverley Park Towers and their mother resigned her position as his hygienist. Though they missed going for rides in the luxurious Chrysler minivan, they didn't miss Dr. Bucknell.

And they were positively buoyant when their father forsook Miss Voorhees' duplex on Farrand Street and came back home to live. All three children said they'd grown weary of so much pizza and ice cream. And how, they wondered, could anyone be so fussy about a little mess, a little disorder, a little cat hair?

According to Mrs. de Valera, who is Irish through and through, Julian still calls the cats Tristan and Isolde. And though she's never been one to gossip, or tell tales out of school, she says she's heard it on good authority that Dr. Bucknell and Miss Voorhees, of all people, are now an item. She says the duplex on Farrand Street is back on the market. She also says that Miss Voorhees and Dr. Bucknell have their names jointly on the waiting list at Apple Crest Condominiums, where pets bigger than budgie birds and children under sixteen are not permitted.

Chapter Nineteen

Sassafras, the Lighthouse Cat

Sassafras was a silver spotted tabby with hazel eyes. Three months of the year, from January to March, she was an indoor cat, living with Tyrone and Jessie Curtis in a snug apartment above Dolph's Hardware on Bay Street. But from mid-April till the close of navigation in December, she was a lighthouse cat on

Trowbridge Island. Here, her duties included helping Tyrone tend the light, welcoming visitors, and keeping the island's mouse population under control. During her long life, although she took all three jobs seriously, mouse management was probably her first priority.

By the time Tyrone and Jessie acquired her, Sassafras had already produced two litters of kittens. In her early years, she was owned by Tyrone's sister, Eileen, who said she knew of no other cat who engendered such varicoloured offspring. In her last batch alone there had been a red one, a brown one, a striped and two mackerels, with a corresponding variety in eye colour. It made you wonder, Eileen said, just what kind of night life Sassafras had been leading.

That all came to an end, though, when Eileen's husband was transferred to Vancouver. At first, they debated taking Sassafras with them. The trouble was, they knew people who had tried that, had put their cat in the car and driven to Calgary, and then when they arrived at their destination, the cat had disappeared and was never seen again. They knew of other people who had drugged their cat and put it on an airplane, in the baggage compartment, and when they disembarked at the other end, the cat was dead.

And so that is why Tyrone and Jessie adopted Sassafras, even though they weren't sure how she'd adapt to living nine months of the year on a remote island in Lake Superior. Not that she'd have much choice, once installed: it would either be stay or swim.

As it turned out, Sassafras, or Sass, for short, adapted very well. It was as though she'd been born to the beacon life. After a trip to the Vet's for modification, she joined Tyrone and Jessie for a short voyage to Trowbridge Island aboard the supply ship, *Alexander*

Henry. Snug in her wicker basket, she was blissfully unaware of being out on the high seas.

The first lighthouse Tyrone and Jessie ever tended was the one at Point Porphry. From there they went to Lamb Island, then to Angus Island, and finally to Trowbridge. In the early years, when everything was done by hand, they'd had an assistant, whose job it was to polish the reflectors, paint the light tower and maintain the diesel generator. But then later, as things became automated, there were just the two of them. The foghorn came on by itself, a photoelectric cell operated the light. By the time Sassafras the cat came into their lives, their nine-month stint on Trowbridge was more like a paid holiday. True, they had to call in weather reports on the radio twice a day, make sure the light was flashing and the foghorn working. But nowadays they had a satellite dish for T.V., a freezer, a microwave, and best of all, indoor plumbing. Still, while these modern inventions made life easier and the job a breeze, Tyrone and Jessie began to wonder if the day might come when machines took over completely, when their presence would no longer be required. It was not a pleasant thought.

Sassafras first set on foot on Trowbridge one cool April morning, when there were still patches of snow on the island and ice floes drifting by. Tyrone carried her basket up from the landing stage and placed it on the front porch of the house. When he opened it, Sass sat blinking, looking around, obviously dismayed. The banging and crashing and jostling on the boat had been bad enough, but where was she now? And who were all these sailors patting her on the head? She had no idea whose quaint white house this was, or what she was

doing there. Where were all the traffic noises she was used to, the people hurrying by, the smells and sounds of the hardware store down below? She wasn't sure she liked this place, wherever it was, perched on a rocky, shrub-covered atoll, surrounded by water, exposed to endless sky and blustery winds. But then she noticed a flock of toothsome chickadees in a nearby thicket, could hear squirrels, crows and sea gulls. So the place was inhabited after all. And those rustlings in the dry grass might need further investigation. Was it possible they were being made by rodents? She hadn't had a good feed of fresh mouse in ages.

While Tyrone and a crewman from the *Alexander Henry* went down to the power house and started the diesel generator, and while Jessie lit the stove and began unpacking boxes, Sassafras set herself the task of exploring the house. She checked upstairs and down, went into all the strange-smelling rooms, with their cobwebs and dead moths and furniture covered in newspapers. Then she went outdoors, sniffed through the weedy vegetable garden, whose soil was barely soft enough to scratch. She sharpened her claws on a scrawny birch tree, climbed halfway up a cedar. From there she could look around and survey her kingdom. More water than land in sight. No roads, no streets, no hardware stores. This might take some getting used to. Strange new smells assailed her nostrils. The wind ruffled her fur. It suddenly occurred to her that no one was issuing orders that she stay in the house. It appeared they didn't care. Such freedom made her positively giddy. She jumped out of the cedar, ran helter-skelter to the edge of the cliff, gazed down at the *Alexander Henry* preparing to set sail. She could hear sailors shouting farewell, could see them waving. It was all rather confusing, but interesting. Then she heard Jessie calling her from the door of the house. Something about lunch. Come to think of it, she was ravenous. Crouched at the starting block like a sprinter, she took off in a flurry, leapt a saxifrage bush in a single bound, scared up a pair of courting nuthatches. "Here she comes now," she heard Tyrone say. "I believe she's settling in quite nicely."

It was true—Sassafras did settle in quite nicely. Which is not to say that she was frivolous, or took her duties lightly. She followed Tyrone on his rounds of inspection, up to the light tower, down to the pump house. As the weather warmed, she helped Jessie in the garden. On a mild May evening, she caught her first mouse, brought it in and showed it to everybody, ate it with obvious relish in front of the television set. From then on, she dined on succulent mice anytime she felt a craving. Though she also brought in beetles, grasshoppers and various other crawling fauna, they were more for show—she rarely ate them. And when, on calm, warm summer afternoons, Tyrone and Jessie went for a boat ride in their little punt, or searched nearby beaches for agates and driftwood, Sassafras dutifully stayed home and guarded the island. She could be seen on the rocky outcrop above the boat cove, where the derrick for lifting supplies used to stand, and she would keep a sharp eye out for buccaneers. True, she occasionally dozed off in the sun and slept the afternoon away, but mainly she was vigilant. In all her seasons on Trowbridge, never once did a hostile landing party succeed in surprising her.

The only real change to this annual routine was when the *Alexander Henry* was decommissioned and sent to Kingston as a floating museum. After that, Tyrone and Jessie were transported to and from Trowbridge Island by helicopter. The day before the first such flight, they went to Pet World and purchased a sturdy plastic cat carrier for Sassafras, with front grill and air holes, in which she rode safely and comfortably, but not without complaint. Indeed, her protestations were clearly audible, even over the rattle and roar of the helicopter's engine. Upon arrival at Trowbridge after that first flight, she emerged from the carrier with wild eyes and fur on end. As soon as she realized where she was, she flew like a grey streak up the winding staircase to the light tower and did not come down till the next day.

Never having seen a domestic animal run that fast, the young helicopter pilot, preparing to climb back into his machine, said, "What the hell was that?"

"That was our cat, Sassafras," Jessie informed him. "Nothing personal, but I'm afraid she prefers boat travel."

Just as Tyrone and Jessie had feared, the day came when that same helicopter brought technicians whose job it was to fully automate Trowbridge Lighthouse. It was happening all around the Great Lakes, had already taken place on the West Coast. In the fall of that year, they received official word from the Coast Guard that they were being terminated. "We thank you for your years of service," the letter said, "and wish you a happy and well deserved retirement."

"They make it sound like it was our idea," Tyrone said, struggling to contain his bitterness. "Happy retirement, my arse."

From then until the end of navigation, they spent

quiet afternoons walking familiar paths for the last time, sitting in the evening on the rocks above the boat-cove, watching the spectacular sunsets. That was what Jessie said she'd miss most—the autumn sunsets. Snow fell at the end of October that year, the resident song-birds left early, flocks of Canada geese headed south with what seemed like unaccustomed haste. By early November, with the trees bare and snow on the ground, Tyrone said he felt in his bones that it was going to be a long, hard winter. There were fewer ships than usual going by, and the ones that passed looked ghostly in the mist. Sassafras appeared to sense the sombre mood of her companions. She seldom went outdoors, preferring instead to spend her time sleeping. "She's not as young as she used to be," Tyrone observed. Indeed, it was as though old age had suddenly caught up to all three of them. They lacked the energy and spirit to do things that until then had given them pleasure. Instead, they sat and looked at television, and read books, and occasionally snapped at each other, which was something they'd never done before.

In December they returned to the city by helicopter, took up residence again in their snug apartment above Dolph's Hardware on Bay Street. And sure enough, just as Tyrone had predicted, the snow and bitter cold came early. By Christmas it was like living in Siberia. The wind howled, drifts piled high, the days darkened. And yet, it was not so much the gloom of winter that weighed heavily on them, but rather the thought that come April, for the first time in years, they would not be returning to their beloved lighthouse on Trowbridge Island. Tyrone began to complain of headaches, sore legs, insomnia, shortness of breath. If he went out at all during the day, it was only to stand for a few minutes with the oldtimers in front of the Finlandia Club, listening to them complain. In January, when the bitter northerlies set in and the sun did not climb above the ice fog in the harbour till noon, he sometimes went for coffee with them to the Hoito, but couldn't help feeling like an outsider. In February he began going to the Royalton Hotel after lunch and drinking beer. Some days he'd forget to come home for supper, and it would be pitch dark before Jessie and Sassafras heard him climbing the stairs.

One day he told them he'd been invited to join the Masonic Lodge, and Jessie was happy for him, thinking it might lift him out of his depression. But after the first few meetings he stopped going. He said he didn't understand what it was they were trying to accomplish, or what they wanted from him. He said he'd come to the conclusion that he wasn't a joiner of groups, that perhaps he'd been a reclusive, free-spirited lighthouse keeper too long.

As usual during the winter months, Jessie found comfort in attending church. There was a time when Tyrone used to go with her, but now he didn't. He said that any religion he needed he'd get from T.V. But when she came home after service, she'd find him sound asleep in front of some blaring, confrontational talk show. During the week she helped out at bake sales and rummage sales, and collected tinned goods for Shelter House. She joined a sewing circle, went to teas, spent afternoons at the library teaching English to immigrants. Three evenings a week she visited Bethany Retirement Home and played cards with the pensioners, or sat and listened to their life stories. "Someday," she said, "if I ever find time, I should write a book."

It's been ten years now since Jessie herself went to live at Bethany. She shares a sunny room in the west wing with old Mrs. Ainsworth, a retired school teacher. She says she thinks that had she and Tyrone been able to return to Trowbridge lighthouse, he might have lived several more years. As it was, after their first summer above Dolph's hardware, he more or less gave up. She says it was a sad thing to watch, because though she loved him as much as ever, she couldn't seem to find a way to cheer him, to give him hope. Like Sassafras when her time came, he simply stopped eating. Then he stopped talking, except to complain about lightheadedness and pains in his chest and intestines. Day and night he would lie in bed, with Sassafras beside him, staring at the ceiling. Even with the window open and the room flooded with birdsong, neither he nor his cat responded. It was, says Jessie, as if they were willing themselves to die, and though they both seemed at peace, it broke her heart, especially when she remembered how happy they'd once been. She says she gave up trying to get Tyrone to see a doctor. Twice she sent for a VON nurse, and both times was told that unless he made a valiant effort, her husband would soon have to be hospitalized. One day, before she went out, he called her to his bedside and told her he loved her. He said he wouldn't have traded their years together for anything, and that having thought things over, he was going to try and get better. He drank a little orange juice, told her again he loved her, and fell into a light sleep.

When she came home, he was unconscious. She phoned for an ambulance, and when it arrived, two paramedics, a man and a woman, came running up the stairs with a stretcher. They felt for Tyrone's pulse, put a stethoscope to his chest. Then while the man performed futile CPR on him, the woman led Jessie out of the room and told her she must prepare herself for the worst. They took Tyrone down and put him in the ambulance, and Jessie rode with him to the hospital. When they got there they wheeled him in, and a young doctor, who looked hardly more than a teenager, came and examined him and pronounced him dead.

It took time and the sympathetic support of friends, but eventually Jessie recovered from her loss. Summoning strength she didn't know she possessed, she nursed Sassafras during the faithful old cat's final weeks, made her as comfortable as possible, sat with her on her lap at the open window, so they could feel the breeze on their faces and smell the rain. On foggy days they could hear ships hooting in the harbour and the distant, mournful foghorn out on the breakwater. Then one morning Sassafras did not wake up, and Jessie knew it was time to go to Bethany. It was there, as a matter of fact, that she met a crotchety old man named Honneger, and a personable grey cat named Armadillo.

Chapter Twenty

And Then There Were Four

When Kate and Tony got married, they had no intention of owning a cat. Neither of them had been raised in a pet-oriented family. Admittedly, one winter, Tony and his brother Cosmo had looked after the neighbour's dog, a yapping poodle named Bridget.

But the task had sorely tried their patience. For one thing, Bridget, or Biddy, as the neighbours called her, refused to go for walks. Or, for that matter, to leave the house. She was afraid of the dark, the mailman and loud noises. Her owners might have taken her to Florida with them, had they remembered to get her vaccinated against rabies in time, and had the condo they'd rented at Fort Lauderdale permitted dogs.

A week after Kate and Tony's first wedding anniversary, Kate's aunt Fiona died of heart failure. Her executrix, Kate's older sister, Jill, took care of things in her usual efficient way. She arranged the funeral, went over the will with Fiona's lawyer, distributed Fiona's jewelry and knickknacks according to her wishes. The only thing she had trouble with was the placement of Fiona's cat, a mature orange female named Mimi. It wasn't that Fiona had forgotten about Mimi, it was just that she hadn't expected the cat to outlive her. Because, you see, while Aunt Fiona had looked after herself, had taken flu shots, vitamins and regular exercise, Mimi the cat had never subscribed to what one might call a health-conscious lifestyle. Longevity had never been high on her list of priorities. It's doubtful she ever thought about it. Thanks to her predilection for fattening foods, such as chocolate cake and ice cream, she was overweight, sedentary, and had a history of bothersome ailments, such as fur balls, ear mites, round worms and sneezing. Regarding the latter, cold drafts made her sneeze, as did sunshine and unfamiliar odours. Her main concerns, though, the ones to which she devoted much time and effort, were filling her stomach, making herself beautiful, and finding secluded places to nap. The ringing of the doorbell and telephone annoyed her, and if her litter box went untended, she was apt to show her displeasure by using Fiona's favourite chair as a scratching post. Or, if she were truly vexed, she might heave up a fur ball on the dining room table.

Aunt Fiona was barely cold in her grave when Kate's sister Jill let it be known that she didn't want Mimi the cat. For one thing, she knew Mimi's reputation. For another, she had a small baby to look after, and she'd heard it on good authority that cats, especially older female cats, motivated perhaps by jealousy or inverted maternal instinct, sometimes snuffed the breath out of babies.

"I'm not taking the cat," she told Kate. "And that's final."

"This could pose a problem," Kate said.

"It could, dear sister, except that there's no one else but you, and so the problem is solved. You get the cat."

"I'm not sure I want the cat."

"Consider it your duty."

"I'll have to ask Tony."

"Don't ask him. Tell him."

And that, gentle reader, is how Kate and Tony got their first cat, Mimi.

Since they were both away at work all day, and since they had a small, fenced back yard, and since right off the bat Mimi let it be known that she liked gardens, Kate had a carpenter come and install a cat door. It worked perfectly. On nice days, and during the night, and especially toward morning, or any other time, Mimi could exit for a breath of fresh air without having to resort to shrill commands, the way she did when she wanted food. She enjoyed sniffing flowers and rooting through dead leaves, pretending to be on safari. On occasion, she would waltz in with a moth or grasshopper in her teeth and let it go, as though eager to share her catch. Kate and Tony hoped there were no rats in the garden, and that the ground sparrows would stay out of harm's way.

Even on chilly days that first winter, Mimi would make use of her cat door. After the first dusting of snow, she went out and walked in it, and came back in with a puzzled look and a pink nose.

One blizzardy night in December, a week before Christmas, she went out on patrol, then rushed back in, meowing. "It's too nippy for her," Tony said. "A smart cat would realize that and stay by the fire."

Moments later, Mimi repeated the performance, only this time her voice was louder, more shrill, more urgent. "Kate," Tony said, "why don't you go and see what she wants?"

"Why don't *you?*" Kate answered.

"Well, technically, she's not my cat. She's your cat."

And so the next time Mimi departed, muttering to herself about stupid humans who didn't understand cat language and weren't about to stir themselves and lend a hand, Kate got up and looked out the window. She couldn't believe her eyes. "You'd never guess, Tony," she said. "There's another cat out there."

"Impossible," Tony said, putting down his newspaper, getting to his feet.

But sure enough, there at the end of the garden, huddled among the dead daffodils, was a half-grown black kitten. So Kate opened the door and they went out and got him. He made no fuss when Tony picked him up, brushed snow off his fur and carried him into the house. He stood in the middle of the floor, shivering, meowing softly, hovered over by Mimi, who walked around and around him like an anxious parent, sniffing at him, her eyes wide with puzzlement.

"How do you suppose he got into the garden?" Kate wondered. "And on a night like this."

Tony had no answer. "Makes you wonder. Unless he climbed the fence. Or an overhanging tree. Or found a hole somewhere."

"But if there was a hole, you'd think Mimi would have found it and escaped long ago."

"Mimi is neither stupid nor adventurous. Why would she want to escape?"

So they warmed the black kitten, gave him a drink and a meal, and sat there wondering where he'd come from. After her initial enthusiasm, and perhaps feeling she'd done all she could, Mimi pretty well lost interest. She seemed to say, "Big deal. He's not really much of a cat, is he? If he stays, don't expect me to look after him, because I've got my hands full as it is. Just make sure he knows his place. If there's one thing I can't stand, it's upstarts with delusions of grandeur."

Next day Kate and Tony phoned CKPR, and put an ad in the *Chronicle-Journal*, and asked their neighbours if they knew whose cat it was. All to no avail. No one had lost a cat. No one answered their ad in the newspaper. A week went by, then two weeks, then it was New Year's, and still no one had claimed the black kitten. So, since he seemed to have settled in quite nicely and wasn't picky about his food or where he slept, and deferred to Mimi in matters of protocol and household management, they named him Gus and gave him a shoe box with an old towel in it for his private domain.

And that, gentle reader, believe it or not, is how Kate and Tony acquired their second cat.

Their third cat, Achilles, came from Shelter House, in Fort William, where Tony helped out on weekends serving hot soup to homeless men and women. On occasion, he was even allowed to make the soup, from his favourite recipe of six beans and smoked ham, in a giant cauldron on the gas stove. At three o'clock the front doors would be opened and the drifters would pile in, some of them unshaven and hollow-eyed, others coming down off binges, still others simply hungry and short of funds. The one thing they all had in common was loneliness. They would sit at long tables and have their hearty soup and day-old bread from Parnell's Bakery, and after the meal many of them would while away the hours, drinking coffee, talking, hoping to be able to spend the night.

One October afternoon, a dirty, white, short-haired kitten was found crouched under the Shelter House stairs, and despite the rules against animals, except for seeing-eye dogs, someone let it in. At first it ran and hid in the cloak room. Eventually it came out, obviously frightened, yet, like everybody else, drawn by the prospect of a meal and a warm place to rest. Unfortunately, the new arrival was made to feel less than welcome by a toothless, sour old man named Leon, who had a veritable phobia about cats. People called him Leon Trotsky, because he was always speechifying, trying to stir up unrest, urging revolt against the system. He complained about the food at Shelter House, the hard beds, the lukewarm showers. Nothing pleased him. At least not until he'd had his second or third bowl of soup. It may have been the white kitten's helplessness that annoyed him, its meekness and lack of revolutionary zeal. Before anyone could stop him, he took off one of his boots and threw it, narrowly missing his target.

That was when Tony, busy ladling out six-bean soup, noticed the black patches on the kitten's hind legs, down near its heels, and made the observation that a good name for it would be Achilles. People looked at him blankly, as though naming a stay cat Achilles made no sense to them. Before Leon could throw his other boot, Tony gave him a mug of coffee and stood in front of him, obstructing his view, preventing him from taking aim.

That night, they put Achilles outdoors, but next day he was back, dirtier than ever. He was also very skittish, as anyone would be, having boots flung at them, when all they wanted was a bowl of soup.

Next day Tony asked Kate how she'd feel about a third cat in the house. She said that having an extra mouth to feed would not strain their budget, but that the parties to ask would be Mimi and Gus, the two resident cats, who by now had worked out an amicable division of assets. While not exactly thrilled with each other's company, neither did they come to blows or require serious mediation. "If you think they'll accept this newcomer," Kate said, "and if you think he'll be happy here, why not bring him along? It's apparent he can't stay where he is. Sooner or later, Leon Trotsky's aim will improve."

And so that's what Tony did. He brought Achilles home in a cardboard box and snuck him surreptitiously into the house while Gus and Mimi were asleep. The first thing he and Kate did was give Achilles a bath, with soap and warm water, which Achilles did not appreciate. Then they dried him off, dusted him with flea powder, rewarded him with a tin of Miss Mew tuna, which he ingested like a vacuum sweeper. Only

then did they do what had to be done and present him to his housemates.

In retrospect, it might have been too soon, too sudden. It was not a promising first meeting. All three animals bared fangs, flattened ears and put on a display of hissing. Gus and Mimi, original signatories to a non-aggression pact, quite forgot the terms of their treaty and spit in each other's faces. To restore peace, the combatants were separated and Achilles was banished to the spare bedroom, at whose door Gus and Mimi took turns standing guard, in case this new kid, this brash, albino intruder, tried to escape.

Next day, at Kate's suggestion, Achilles was introduced to Gus and Mimi separately. This worked much better, and after only minor unpleasantries, with gentle urging from the referees, noses were sniffed in a civilized manner and earlier name-calling watered down. There followed an hour or two of standoffishness, of back-turning, during which each cat was studiously ignored by the other two. Gus retired to his shoe box in the hall, from which vantage point he kept an eye on Achilles. Mimi went out into the garden to think things over and get used to the idea of this pale, immature addition to the family. Which left Achilles free to perform a methodical inspection of the house, from top to bottom. He found and used the litter box in the basement, seemed reasonably pleased with his lunch of Tender Vittles. Then, weary from all this unaccustomed social intercourse, and keeping a wary eye on Mimi, who had come back in from gardening and was perched imperiously on the back of the living room sofa, he went and sat at Tony's feet. Demonstrating the affability that was to become his trademark, he put out a paw and tweaked the toe of Tony's sock, as though it were a plaything.

"Look at that," Kate said. "He thinks of you as his benefactor."

"As well he should," Tony said, picking Achilles up, carrying him over to the sofa, placing him as far away from Mimi as possible.

And that gentle reader, is how Kate and Tony, without really meaning to, expanded into a three-cat family.

The following year was an eventful one for them. In March, Kate gave birth to their first daughter, whom they named Gina, after Tony's mother. Contrary to what Kate's sister Jill had once predicted, all three resident cats dutifully refrained from snuffing the baby's breath out of her body. Indeed, once their initial curiosity had been satisfied and they had determined that this new squalling creature was no threat to their collective well-being, they pretty much ignored her. In time they got used to her crying at odd hours, and since she never once followed them down to the basement, or out the cat door into the garden, they were quite prepared to grant her custody of the spare bedroom. Really, the only one to take more than a passing interest in baby Gina was the fourth cat, Peter-Built, a chunky, charcoal grey shorthair with yellow eyes, who arrived in April.

Tony named him Peter-Built because the first time he saw him, crouched on their front doorstep one rainy, miserable night, all hunched up and squared-off, with ears flattened and eyes like little foglamps, he resembled a stocky, Peter-Built truck tractor. Their neighbour across the street, Mrs. Booker, a busybody if ever there was one, had phoned to tell them that one of their cats was locked out in the rain, and wasn't this cruel, in such evil weather. Which Kate and Tony found hard to believe, because at that very moment, Mimi, Gus and Achilles were all in plain view, scattered about the living room on various chairs and couches, snoring their heads off, oblivious to the wind and rain beating against the windows.

So Tony opened the front door, and sure enough, there on the top step was a dark, furry object, which immediately got up and scurried away. At first, Tony wasn't sure it had been a cat. But when he looked out again later, he could see that the nosy widow Booker across the street had been right—there was indeed a soggy cat on their doorstep. So he opened the door slowly, and made reassuring noises, and this time, though the cat didn't flee, it went down two steps and sat there, cowering.

"This is ridiculous," Tony told Kate. "Somebody's grey cat is out there in the rain."

"It might be best not to invite it in," Kate said. "If that's what you had in mind. What we don't need just now is another stray."

"But the poor thing is dripping wet."

"It will soon realize it's at the wrong house and go home. Trust me."

When Tony looked out again an hour later, the cat was still there, thoroughly soaked, looking like a muskrat. He could also see that it was shivering. Having been through a similar scenario with black Gus, he wondered why this new, yellow-eyed vagrant had chosen their house. Did it sense that there were other cats inside? Was some strange telepathy at work?

When Tony looked out a third time, the cat was gone. But then, halfway through Gina's bath, the phone rang. It was Mrs. Booker across the street again, who warned that if they didn't let their cat in our of the rain, she intended to report them to the Humane Society first thing in the morning.

"It's not our cat," Tony informed her. "Besides, it's gone."

"No," said Mrs. Booker, "it's not gone. It's still there. I can see it. And if it's not your cat, whose is it?"

"I have no idea," Tony said. "I've never laid eyes on it before."

"Neither have I. I assumed it was yours."

"Well, it isn't. Our cats are all indoors, as we speak."

"It seems to me you could let it in anyway. You shouldn't leave an animal outdoors on a night like this."

"But when I open the door, it runs away. It's afraid of me."

"Nonsense," scoffed Mrs. Booker. "You just don't know how to do it. You should put down some food for it, entice it in with kindness. It's a terrible night to be alone."

"So why don't you put out some food and entice it into your house?"

"Oh, I couldn't do that, young man. No, I'm in no position to do that. Not at my age. Not when I have Jimmy, my little parakeet, here in his cage. He'd be scared to death."

So finally Tony put a dish of Mimi's Fancy Feast on the floor in the front hall, and leaving the door open, sat back and waited. A few minutes later the grey cat put his head in, then his shoulders, then the rest of him, and after gobbling a mouthful of food ran back out in the rain. He was a little less stealthy the next time, and stayed longer, eating as fast as he could and sizing things up with his slitted yellow eyes.

"He's really quite handsome," Kate observed. "Or he could be, if he weren't so thin. You can see his ribs. And look, he seems to be wearing some kind of necklace."

"I think it's the remnants of an old flea collar," Tony said. "But I don't see any tag."

It was at that moment that Gus woke up, saw the intruder, and yowled. Which of course woke Mimi and Achilles. For a moment there was stunned inertia. Then, in her role as matriarch and doyenne of the pride, Mimi came down off her chair, hissing and spitting, slinking low to the ground, growling deep in her throat. Halfway to the door she gave Kate and Tony a withering look, as though asking, "Who's in charge of security around here? Why aren't you two defending the fort instead of just sitting there?"

It occurred to Tony that had he wanted to, the grey cat could very well have stood his ground and challenged Mimi. But he didn't. Evidently deciding that discretion was the better part of valour, he withdrew. But not very far. From where he sat, Tony could see him crouched near the door, peering in, as though loath to leave the warmth. But then, as the rain had stopped, and as the other two cats had joined Mimi in a loose line of defence, he must have decided that now was as good a time as any to take his leave. One moment he was there, the next he was gone, and Mimi looked very pleased with herself. She sniffed the floor, inspected the empty food dish, and only when she was sure this latest interloper had been repulsed did she sound the all clear and climb back into her chair. She didn't close her eyes, though. Nor did Gus and Achilles. All three remained vigilant, glancing from the door to Kate and

Tony, perhaps doubting what they'd just witnessed.

"Did you see the size of that monster?" black Gus probably said. "It's a good thing I spotted him, barging in on us like that, uninvited."

"Did you notice the colour of his eyes?" Achilles no doubt added. "The eyes of a bully."

But Mimi only snickered. "Take my word for it, he's a grey marshmallow. His type doesn't impress me. Did you see how he turned tail when I told him to buzz off?"

As you might guess, the cats' complacency was short-lived. The very next night, Peter-Built was back. Again Tony gave him a dish of Fancy Feast just inside the door, and again he wolfed it down. This time, though, he didn't run when Mimi came down off her chair. Just as Kate was in the midst of saying, "Tony, you'd better be ready to break up a fight here," Peter-Built did the most amazing thing either of them had ever seen a cat in crisis do. He rolled over on his back, exposing his throat and abdomen. It was as though he were saying, "You have me outnumbered. I'm too weary, too hungry, too sick to fight and I'm tired of running. If you intend to beat me up, go ahead. But I'd rather not leave. These nights in the rain have used up the last of my will. And this looks like a good place, with kind people and tolerant cats. At least I hope you're tolerant. Right now, you look rather inhospitable. Please tell me it's all show."

To be truthful, Mimi, Gus and Achilles appeared a bit flummoxed. How could you properly intimidate and expel someone who was lying on his back in a posture of surrender, whimpering about what a hard life he'd been leading? They took turns sniffing his tail, his ears, his sheathed claws. Kate, who was busy preparing Gina's bottle, said he looked like Gulliver surrounded by Lilliputians.

"What's that stupid thing you've got around your neck?" Mimi no doubt asked. "Some kind of decoration?"

Peter-Built sighed with exasperation. "The remains of a flea collar," he probably said. "Someone, I forget who, put that on me a long time ago. I wish I could get it off."

"Will he let you touch him?" Kate wondered.

And so Tony knelt down among the Lilliputians and for the first time ever, despite Mimi's warning to be careful, touched Peter-Built. He touched him on the shoulder, stroked his head, and all Peter-Built did was close his eyes. Again he seemed to be saying, "I'm too tired to run. If you want to throw me out, go ahead."

But of course they didn't throw him out. Not and risk having the widow Booker, who owned a parakeet named Jimmy, report them to the S.P.C.A. As they had done for Gus and Achilles, they gave him a box with an old bath towel in it and his own food dish, and when he realized he was being allowed to stay, he got up and crept unobtrusively about the entire house, staying out of people's way, not making a sound, closely followed by Gus, who seemed intrigued by him and only hissed once or twice.

"Would you look at that," Kate said. "He's not ornery after all. It's like he'd been expecting this. I wonder where he came from, and why he chose us? It's uncanny."

Of course next day they put an ad in the newspaper, and phoned the radio station, but as with black Gus, there was no response. They really hadn't expected any. When Tony told Kate the new cat's name was Peter-Built, Kate said she had no intention of calling him that.

"I'll call him Peter," she said, snipping off his tattered flea collar. "Or just plain Pete. But not Peter-Built."

And though it took time for everyone to get adjusted to his presence, to sort out who would sleep where and who would eat first, Peter-Built turned out to be the gentlest cat of all. When asked to, he would mediate tiffs between Gus and Achilles, who sometimes let sibling rivalry get out of hand. If Mimi were otherwise occupied, Peter-Built would step in and separate the combatants. Speaking of Mimi, he held her in the highest esteem. He never tried to usurp her space or steal her windowsill. He stayed clear of her when she was in one of her moods. Though he was big and chesty and had compelling eyes, he was, as Mimi had accurately predicted, a marshmallow underneath.

Though the other cats often went out in the garden and used the soft soil as their litter box, and even sharpened their claws on the fence posts, Peter-Built seldom did. Indeed, he showed little interest in the outdoors. On rainy days, or snowy days, or days when the wind blew, he stayed in bed, perfectly content.

Peter-Built's chief distinction, though, was his attachment to baby Gina. Almost from the start, he bonded with her, stayed close to her, allowed her to probe his ears and poke her small fingers into his belly fur. He even let her pull his tail. In his eyes, she could do no wrong. While Mimi, Gus and Achilles tended to ignore her and keep their distance from her grasping, inquisitive hands, Peter-Built often slept in her room, sometimes on her bed, and when she was feverish with the sniffles or fretful with colic, he never left her side.

And that, gentle reader, is how, incredible as it may seem, Kate and Tony ended up with four cats. I wish I could say they all lived happily ever after, but unfortunately, I can't. A month before their second daughter, Amanda, was born, Mimi, at age fifteen, died of heart failure, just as her previous owner, Aunt Fiona, had done. At first Kate and Tony thought she'd eaten something disagreeable in the garden, but when they took her to the Vet, they learned the truth. And so Mimi is no longer with them. A year ago they moved to a larger house on the Court Street Ridge, with a nice view of the Sleeping Giant. Of course they took their three cats with them. They said that for the first week Gus hid in the basement, Achilles in a kitchen cupboard, Peter-Built under Gina's bed. But then one day all three emerged from their hiding places, enjoyed a copious meal, and, as sibling cats invariably do, went about laying claim to furniture and advantageous window-sills. These days, while Gus and Achilles wrestle in the sun on the living room floor, or gaze serenely out at the harbour, yellow-eyed Peter-Built, in his role as nanny, has his paws full, keeping tabs on two very active little girls.

Chapter Twenty-One

Good Golly, Miss Molly!
or: Let Sleeping Dogs Lie

This story goes back a good many years. It takes place at Pigeon River during the War. To be exact, at S.S. #2 Pardee, a mile this side of the U.S. border, not far from Devon Road. My mother was the school teacher there, with all grades in one room but seldom more than nine or ten pupils. Since my father was away at the War, my mother and I were on our own. We lived in a rambling old farmhouse, of which one entire wing, formerly the parlour and veranda, had been expanded and renovated to make a classroom. New windows had been installed, along with a wood-burning heater, a blackboard and a dozen desks. We had no electricity, no running water, no telephone. What we had was a twenty-foot well in the back yard, which bore a skim of ice in winter and in the spring was full of mosquito larvae. Our fuel supply was a pile of dry poplar logs in the back yard, which it was my job to saw, split and stack in the woodshed. The only lights we had were Aladdin coal oil lamps. The only plumbing was an outdoor biffy, which my mother referred to as "the comfort station." We had no refrigeration, and so most of our victuals, except for canned food, came from local farmers and our vegetable garden. We got milk, eggs, butter and the occasional chicken from one farmer, ducks and rabbits (when we could afford them) from another. Every Saturday, my mother stoked the kitchen range and baked bread in its capacious oven, sometimes a cake and cookies, on special occasions, cranberry tarts.

Despite chimney fires, drafty floors, frozen wells and chilly trips to the outhouse, we learned to cope. It was, after all, an adventure. At least for me it was. I had the nearby woods to explore, the old abandoned farm buildings to play in. Hardly a day went by that I didn't discover new animal tracks, new birds, new insects. On weekends I visited the distant homes of my classmates.

For Toby, my black and white cat, it was a marvellous era of staying out all night and preying upon the plentiful mice and chipmunks. Though he remained a staunch indoor cat, with a fondness for the hearth, he loved the great outdoors too, almost as much as I did.

When it was time to work on the poplar logs, which was practically every day, I could count on him to at least sit and watch. He may have associated wood with warmth.

For my mother, a strong, brave woman, those years could not have been easy. Besides her heavy load of school work and the arduous living conditions, there was the constant worry about my father. For it was, after all, wartime. I remember how we listened attentively to news broadcasts on our battery radio and followed the progress of the armies on a tattered map of Europe. I also remember how we looked forward to my father's letters, which stopped abruptly in June of 1944, when he was killed on the beach at Normandy.

Before we went to Pigeon River, Toby's experience with dogs was minimal. In his first few years, he really hadn't encountered any. And so he was less than thrilled to discover that two of my mother's pupils, Gareth and Diane, owned a large, friendly golden Lab named Molly. The two children, one in grade four, the other in grade five, lived several miles up Devon Road. It was too far to walk, too far to bike, especially in bad weather, and so they hitched their old brown semi-retired Clydesdale, Ernie, to a buckboard and rode to school like Hutterites. In the dead of winter, when Devon Road was unplowed and impassable, Ernie, wearing a blanket, would be hitched to a covered sleigh with a small tin stove in it, and though he would arrive with frosted nostrils and icicles hanging from his lower lip, his two passengers would be snug and warm. As he was never in a hurry (indeed, at his age he had only one gait —a slow, steady walk), it took him an hour and a half to cover the distance between home and school. When fresh green grass sprouted along the sides of the road in spring, he often paused for a nibble. He also liked to stop and rest coming up some of the steeper hills. Once or twice a week Gareth and Diane would arrive late, and always blamed Ernie for having taken a breather and dozed off where he stood. As they themselves often caught a little extra shut-eye en route, they wouldn't notice their lack of progress until one of them woke up.

Having reached his destination, Ernie would be un-harnessed and either left to graze in the field or else put into a stall in the old barn, where he would eat oats, drink water and spend the day ruminating about past achievements. I think he would have agreed: it was a good life for a farm horse in the twilight of his career.

The golden Lab, Molly, a gentle, philosophical dog who loved everybody at first sight, always came to school too. She would trot along behind the wagon, making side trips to investigate new or familiar scents, scaring up partridges in the fall. Having been victim-ized by both in the past, she steered well clear of skunks and porcupines. On nice days she would sleep in the sun in the schoolyard, or wander about the fields with Ernie.

As far as Toby was concerned, the problem started the first nasty day in October, when Molly asked to be let in out of the rain. Had she been able to, she would probably have said, "It's fine for Ernie, in his nice dry stall in the horse barn, munching oats and flicking his tail, but for a yellow dog of advanced years, it's no fun."

So Molly came in, shook herself, and lay down in the doorway between the classroom and the kitchen. From there, she could listen to my mother telling us about Magellan and Marco Polo and explaining the intricacies of arithmetic. The only trouble was, my cat Toby liked to spend his forenoons in the classroom too, under the stove, or on a vacant desk, where he could feel a part of things yet be left undisturbed.

On this particular day, finding his access blocked by a large, reclining arch enemy, he was, to say the least, disgruntled. He stood well back, thinking things over. No way around, no way over, no way under. Stalled at the roadblock. Served him right, he probably thought, for not entering the classroom earlier, after recess. And was it his imagination, or had somebody just cleaned out his food dish? He didn't remembering finishing the last of his breakfast. Stymied, nonplussed, he retired behind the woodbox for further cogitation. Meanwhile, the rain fell, the wind blew, and Molly continued to fill the doorway.

Had Toby but known it, Molly posed no threat. She was very used to cats, had three of her own at home, one of whom, an orphan, she'd all but raised. And yes, she'd helped herself to the contents of that dish on the floor. What use to deny it?

A few minutes later, Toby was back. This time he came a bit closer to the sleeping dog, looked pleadingly at my mother. Could she not see that he needed help? Would someone either move the dog out of the way or else lift him over?

Again he retreated, again he returned. It had become a question now of honour. Not of heroics, but of a cat's rights in his own house. And why was everybody too busy to see his plight? Were Marco Polo and improper fractions really that interesting? He somehow doubted it.

The fact is, we were well aware of Toby's predicament. Without seeming to, we were all watching, wondering what he'd do. In another hour it would be lunch time. Hopefully, he'd screw his courage to the sticking place before that and take the plunge, so to speak. But it looked doubtful. You could see that he was longing to come in and join us, but couldn't. He walked away dispiritedly, sniffed at his empty dish. Talk about adding insult to injury. Then he approached the dog again, stood on tiptoes to look over her. What if she woke up just as he made his move? She'd open and close those fierce canine jaws like a crocodile, and there he'd be, caught in midair.

As for me, I knew all along he'd do it. I knew my cat. I knew how badly he wanted to be in the classroom. It's where he spent all his forenoons. And no mangy yellow dog was going to keep him from his appointed place. Besides, he had his reputation to think of.

He took a few steps backward, crouched, wiggled his rump the way I'd often seen him do outdoors, and then, like a circus performer shot from a cannon, catapulted himself through the air. It was as though he'd suddenly grown wings. Never did a cat perform such a daredevil leap. He cleared Molly with miles to spare, like a champion highjumper, and landed with a clatter on the classroom floor. He stood there, looking very pleased with himself, yet nonchalant too, and glanced over his shoulder at the obstacle he'd just hurdled. To his amazement, Molly hadn't been asleep at all. Both her eyes were wide open. She returned his gaze cooly. If he expected praise from her, he'd have to wait a while.

"Next time," she seemed to be saying, "why not just step over me, instead of pretending to be an acrobat on the flying trapeze? I don't even mind if you walk across my paws. Nobody likes a show-off."

We pupils, having witnessed all this, gave Toby a smattering of applause. Pleased, yet ever humble, and with one suspicious eye still on Molly, he stood beside the stove and washed his whiskers. There remained, of course, the quandary of what to do if she were still there when he wanted to leave. He sighed, as did the dog, and lay down for a nap. My mother brought her pre-lunch lesson to a close, began putting insoluble arithmetic questions on the blackboard. This afternoon, she announced, with autumn making its presence felt, we'd get together and study the hibernating habits of bears.

From that day on, whenever Toby found Molly blocking the doorway to the classroom, he'd jump over her with little hesitation. Sometimes he jumped higher than he needed to, sometimes he didn't. It was my feeling that once he knew she wouldn't gobble him up, he wanted to see how close he could come without actually touching her. I think he trusted her, but not blindly, not implicitly. Or perhaps, like athletes in general and cats in particular, he believed in the conservation of energy.

Chapter Twenty-Two

Custer's Last Stand

Custer was a brown farm cat who liked cows. The first time Helvi Chipola saw him was early one frigid winter morning when she went out to the barn and saw what looked like a moth-eaten fur hat on her favourite Holstein's back.

"Well," she said, "what's this we're wearing these days?"

But then she noticed a pair of green eyes at one end of the fur hat, and realized it was a live animal. To be specific, a jowly, full grown, short-haired cat with frostbitten ears and disheveled whiskers. "What have we here?" she said, remembering an old female tabby named Sari, who had also liked to cohabit with livestock, back when she and her late husband, Oscar, were first married.

Helvi and Oscar Chipola had begun wedded life in 1938, a year before the start of World War II. Their farm comprised two hundred and forty acres of verdant pasture land in Scoble Township. They had the tallest silo and largest dairy barn in the district, plus good water from two deep wells and a meandering trout stream. At least Oscar called it a trout stream, though in truth it contained no fish. Trout or otherwise.

In 1939, their first daughter, Arja, was born. Arja was a pudgy, fair-haired, laughing child, who soon grew equally fond of school, animals and the outdoors. In time, she would go away to Guelph Agricultural college and become Scoble Township's first female veterinarian. In 1941, her sister Lea was born. If Oscar and Helvi had been expecting a replica of Arja, they were in for a surprise: Lea was reed-thin, dark-haired and temperamental. She had little fondness for animals, even less for farm life. She seldom if ever went outdoors to play, preferring instead to compose melodies in her head and listen to the radio. At school, though she was a fair student, the only things that interested her were drawing and learning the violin. For the latter she had an inexplicable passion. At least it was inexplicable until Oscar remembered that his maternal grandmother, a resident of Salpausselka, had played first cello in the Helsinki Symphony Orchestra, and in later years had given music lessons.

It was common knowledge that although Oscar had hoped for a son, he adored his two daughters. He used to be impatient for them to wake up in the morning, because he liked listening to them prattle. He took pleasure in pointing things out to them—newborn calves, white rabbits in winter, gamboling ponies in spring. Summer evenings, when he came in from mending fences, he would take them swimming in the creek. He gave them rides on his tractor, took them by truck Sunday afternoons to Chippewa Park, where they threw peanuts to the bears and rode the merry-go-round. When they were old enough, Oscar let them watch a foal being born, and although Lea ran and hid, Arja stared, fascinated, and was first to touch the trembling, steaming offspring.

In the fall of 1944, Oscar went away to war with the Royal Canadian Service Corps, and for several months drove a khaki six-by-six through the mud and dust of northern Italy. In the spring of 1945, on the outskirts of Piacenza, his truck ran off the road in a rainstorm and he hurt his legs and spine. While half the convoy turned east toward Austria and the other half west toward France, Oscar lay in a Genoese hospital, recuperating. Three months later he came home to Scoble Township. Try as he might, though, he could no longer bring himself to care about milk quotas or dairy herds. Instead, he sat in his favourite easy chair drinking beer and let Helvi do all the work. When Arja showed him how well she could ride a horse, he forced himself to watch. When Lea played the violin for him, he didn't smile, he wept. At night, he sometimes called out Italian names in his sleep, and when Helvi asked whose names these were, he said they belonged to fellow invalids. When he called out women's names, Helvi guessed they must be nurses.

Ten years to the day after his return from the War, still in pain, Oscar Chipola hanged himself in the cow barn. He threw a rope over a rafter one Sunday morning when Helvi and her daughters were away at church, and when they came home they found him strangled, slowly turning. The police and coroner were summoned, and a few days later Oscar's death notice appeared in the *Times Journal*. His livestock prizes and Army exploits were listed, but not the manner of his death. His funeral, which under normal circumstances would have been largely attended, was a small, private affair.

That winter, Helvi was very lonely on the farm. Arja had gone away to Guelph. Lea, who was boarding in town and attending Port Arthur Collegiate, came home only on weekends, and then spent most of her time practising the violin. She told Helvi she missed her father as much as anyone did, but had her own ways of showing it.

And then one winter's day Helvi discovered a brown cat sleeping on a cow's back. Where it had come from, she didn't know. She phoned some of her neighbours, but they didn't know either. When she went out to the henhouse later in the day to collect eggs, she was rather surprised to find the cat following in her footsteps. It sat in the snow watching her every movement, and then actually ran ahead of her, so that by the time she reached the kitchen door, carrying her basket of eggs, the cat was there, waiting for her. It accompanied her indoors, and without benefit of invitation walked boldly into the living room, leapt up on a chair beside the space heater and settled itself comfortably. According to Helvi, you would have thought the cat had done this countless times before. It sat there smugly, appraising her with its green, unblinking eyes, as though expecting to be fed. "By the look of you, I'd say you're not a barn cat," Helvi said. "But with your frostbitten ears and broken whiskers, you're not quite a house cat either. Whoever you are, you seem to think you've found a home."

Though it didn't occur to her until later, the chair the cat had chosen, had run and jumped into, was Oscar's favourite chair, the one he'd sat in hour after hour, listening to the radio, close to the stove, trying to get some heat into his bones. For some reason, it was the only chair in the whole house that gave him relief from constant agony.

When Lea came home for the weekend she named the cat Custer, simply because she'd been reading a book about Montana, about the battle of the Little Bighorn, where General Custer had met his fate at the hands of the Sioux in 1876. "The cat looks like he's been in a serious tussle," she said. "I think his name should be Custer."

So Custer the brown cat lived with Helvi for many years, followed her about the farm like a faithful dog, escorted her diligently to the henhouse. And whenever she couldn't find him, she'd look in the barn, and there he'd be, sleeping on a cow's back. In the house, though, his favourite roost was Oscar's old chair beside the space heater—a chair Helvi had almost thrown out ages ago, but for some strange reason, didn't.

The reason I know all this is that Lea Chipola was once a student in my senior English class. Not long ago, she wrote me a nice letter from Kingston, where she lives with her husband and five children and teaches chamber music at Queen's University.

Chapter Twenty-Three

Aunt Ruth & Caliban

From her window under the eaves, Aunt Ruth watches neighbourhood children at play. Their voices rise on the crisp autumn air, in harmony, some- how, with the burnished shafts of sunlight slanting

across the garden. Among signs of summer's end—
dead flowers, bare trees—the children symbolize, at
least to Ruth, exuberant life. Their very presence
double-dares the threat of winter. If anyone can survive
the snowstorms lurking just over the horizon, surely it's
the children.

From her garret, like a sentry, or a lighthouse keeper,
Ruth sees a dark nimbus of cloud gathering beyond the
suburbs, and, higher in the sky, wind-distorted tufts of
cirrus. Mares' tails, she believes they're called. Bad
omens. The rest of the sky is empty. The wrens and
starlings have all flown south. She's pretty sure she saw
the last of them depart a week ago yesterday. By now,
they're probably approaching Mexico. You have to
hand it to the wrens and starlings. They know when it's
time to pack up and leave. Were she able to, she'd fly
to Mexico with them. She'd escape this cheerless apartment under the eaves, this draughty loft in which she
seems destined to spend the rest of her days. As recently as a year ago, she'd contemplated entering a
seniors' home. Her name was on the list at Pioneer
Ridge and at St. Joseph's Heritage. But when Pioneer
Ridge phoned and said they had a room for her, a
shared room, mind you, but a room nevertheless, she
declined the offer. She told them she'd stay where she
was a while longer, living on her own. She said she
wasn't sure she could tolerate a roommate's presence.

"You realize you'll lose your turn on the waiting
list," they warned her.

"So be it," she said.

"Once you cancel, you lose your turn. God knows
when we'll have another vacancy."

"When the next inmate expires?" Ruth suggested,
and heard the line go dead.

Since then, she's had her doubts. She wakes up in the middle of the night, stricken with loneliness, fearing she's made the wrong decision. More than once, the thought of ending it all with sleeping pills has crossed her mind. Lying in bed, she hears tree branches rattling in the wind and freight trains whistling at the edge of town. Lonely sounds. Sounds she might not be aware of living in an old folks' home. If she ever went to Mexico, she'd find a place far from the tracks. Maybe on the beach at Acapulco. Her landlady, Milly, who lives downstairs, once spent a winter in Acapulco. Or was it Veracruz? It might have been Veracruz.

As she watches the children playing in the garden and hears them being called home for supper one by one, she wonders what it must be like to be a mother. Or, at her age, a grandmother. It isn't the first time she's pondered this, though it's been a while. Would bringing babies into the world have given her more satisfaction than spending forty years in a stuffy classroom at Eden Park Elementary School? Quite possibly. Though who's to know? Teaching other people's kids didn't exactly fulfill her, but then again, it didn't break her heart either.

From her attic window, she watches darkness descend. As daylight fades and street lamps come on, she notices the scrawny grey cat that's been skulking about the garden lately. It seems to be a homeless cat. It has a deformed or injured hind leg and walks with a limp. As far as she knows, nobody in the neighbourhood feeds it. Which may explain why it's been getting thinner and thinner. Before the wrens and starlings left, she used to observe the cat stalking them. It was no contest, really. The cat wasn't nearly fast enough. Nor did it seem to understand the need for stealth. Instead of springing at its prey, it would stumble forward, hampered by its gimpy leg, and watch the intended victim fly away. Had she liked cats better, and if her own arthritic knees had been less painful, Ruth might have taken table scraps or a tin of sardines down to the garden. But it's a long climb up and down those unlit back stairs. Twenty-three steps in all. Besides, let's face it, she prefers birds to cats. Always has.

Looking out her window one morning in December, Ruth notices a layer of frost over everything. The dead raspberry canes have turned white, as have the drooping sunflowers. Nothing, she reflects, is as desolate as a frozen garden. By noon, large snowflakes are falling, and as she sits down for her tea and toast, she notices the grey cat. It sits among dead rhododendrons, skinnier than ever, and you can see its paw prints in the snow. Aloud, Ruth says, "You stupid thing, the birds left long ago." Then she notices a small boy, familiar because of his tousled red hair, emerge from a house on the far side of the street and begin throwing snowballs at the cat. At first, the cat perceives no danger, but then, realizing it's under attack, drags itself in among the raspberry canes. Without meaning to, Ruth raps sharply on the window to attract the boy's attention. When he looks up, she admonishes him by shaking a disapproving finger, and is surprised, not to say shocked, when he sticks his tongue out at her. That's something not even her most recalcitrant pupil ever did. Again without meaning to, she pushes open the window, thrusts her head out in the frosty air. "Stop that, young man!" she shouts. "That's not nice. Why aren't you in school?"

"It's Saturday!" the boy shouts back at her, lobbing

more snowballs. "Anyway, what do you care?"

"I care because that's my cat!"

The boy looks up at her, scoffing. "That's not your cat. It's nobody's cat."

"How would like it if you had a sore leg and someone threw snowballs at you?"

"I'd like it fine. What's it to you? Mind your own business."

By mid-afternoon, snow is falling thickly and the wind has strengthened. Down in the garden, Ruth sees no fresh paw prints, and supposes the cat must still be hiding. Reluctantly, she puts on her coat, ties a scarf over her head, descends the twenty-three steps to the back door. At one time, she reflects, a few years ago, before her knees stiffened, this would have been a breeze. Now, it's a struggle. And sure enough, there, under the sunflowers, the grey cat is curled up, half-covered with snow. At first, Ruth expects it to get to its feet and run for cover under someone's porch. But it doesn't. Momentarily, she wonders if it's dead. That would solve the problem of what to do with it. Leave it there. But the cat isn't dead. At least not quite. Though motionless, its eyes are open. Pale yellow eyes, half hidden by white membrane. When Ruth reaches down to brush snow off its fur, the cat raises its head and emits an ineffectual hiss. "Don't spit at me," Ruth says. "You're in no position to spit at anyone."

Carrying the cat upstairs to her attic apartment, surprised at its lightness, yet feeling the pain in her own knees, Ruth wonders if she's thwarting nature. Maybe the cat doesn't want to be rescued. Maybe it wants to die, expects to die. After wrapping it in a bath towel and placing it on her bed, she sits at the window to finish her tea and toast. Outdoors, she can't help noticing that a full-scale blizzard is in progress. The wind howls like a banshee. Down below, the garden is all but obliterated.

For an hour the cat lies there, staring at her with its pale yellow eyes. She has the peculiar feeling she's being judged, assessed. Then, just as she decides to brew a fresh pot of tea, the cat closes its eyes and falls asleep.

If she expects a show of gratitude, Aunt Ruth is due for disappointment. Lulled by the sounds of the storm and the cat's breathing, she herself dozes off, sitting at the kitchen table. When she wakes up, the first thing she sees is the cat, who has emerged from its towel and is sitting there looking at her. It seems amazingly unafraid. It appears to have no intention of trying to hide or defend itself. And so Ruth opens a tin of salmon, pours a saucer of milk, and places these offerings on the floor. Then she picks the cat up, feeling its ribs and gritty, matted fur, and puts it on the floor too. At first, it just stands there, shivering. Then, very slowly, balancing on three legs, it lowers its face and begins lapping salmon juice. It laps until the juice is all gone, then bites off pieces of salmon and transfers them to the floor. But then, unexpectedly, it topples over on its side, as though exhausted from a long journey.

Watching all this, Ruth says, "It's no wonder you couldn't catch a bird, you pitiful, three-legged wretch. You're nothing but skin and bones."

For the rest of the afternoon, Ruth combs the cat's unkempt fur, washes it with a damp cloth, and all the time she's doing this the cat lies still, flicking the tip of its tail, watching her with its hooded yellow eyes. Its left hind leg, she notices, is limp and crooked. Whenever she touches it, even lightly, the cat growls deep in its throat. "Don't growl at me, mister," Ruth says. "You're in no position to growl at anyone." When she's finished, the cat, looking only marginally better, lowers its head, sighs a deep sigh, and again falls asleep. Ruth reflects that it's what she'd do too, if she were under the weather, or feeling sorry for herself.

These days, Aunt Ruth's cat, whose name, by the way, is Caliban, spends his mornings lying on her window-sill, keeping watch over the neighbourhood. When black-capped chickadees congregate in the garden to peck at frozen sunflowers, he flicks the tip of his tail and chatters. At such moments, Ruth will say, "It's all bluff, Caliban. You know it is. If it wasn't, you'd be down there, covered in feathers, instead of up here, sporting a fancy flea collar, looking out my window."

It may be true. Since the day of the blizzard, Caliban has shown no interest whatsoever in leaving Aunt Ruth's attic apartment. At night, he sleeps at the foot of her bed. When the afternoon sun shines in and warms his fur, or when Aunt Ruth strokes him and tells him he'd be handsome except for his frost-nipped ears and broken whiskers, he purrs. When Debashis, the delivery boy from Habjan's Grocery on Elm Street, climbs the twenty-three steps with the week's provisions and leaves the door ajar, Caliban will limp to the top of the stairwell and gaze down, but that's as far as he goes. He has his litter box in the far reaches of Ruth's hall closet, and though he enjoys a treat of salmon now and then, he seems content at other times to dine on mundane cat food.

If you ask Aunt Ruth where his name came from, she'll tell you that in Shakespeare's *The Tempest*, Caliban is a lame, unsightly creature at whom people throw things, and though harmless, he is scorned by those who underestimate him.

Ruth will also tell you that next spring, when the snow melts and the weather warms, she and Caliban intend to go down in the garden and take their ease among the sunflowers and rhododendrons. They intend to be there, she says, in time to see the first raspberries blossom, and to welcome the wrens and starlings back from Mexico.

Chapter Twenty-Four

The Great Millennium Mount Everest Cat Expedition

It may come as a surprise to many, but in the spring of 2000, to celebrate the new millennium, the Mountaineering Society of the International Cat Federation sent a climbing expedition to the Himalayas. Their goal was the summit of Mount Everest, highest peak on earth, 29,028 feet above sea level, on the border between Nepal and Tibet.

Mount Everest's Tibetan name, *Chomolungma*, means "Goddess Mother of the World." It can be reached from two directions: from the north, through China and Tibet, or from the south, through India and Nepal. Since the Second World War, most expeditions have assailed the mountain from the south. Some have been successful, some have not. In 1953, as everyone knows, Hillary and Tenzing, the first mortals to conquer Everest, did it from the south. Before the War, attacks on Everest had been launched mainly from the north. None, so far as is known, was successful, although it is thought that two British climbers, Mallory and Irvine, might have reached the summit in 1924, on their third attempt. Unfortunately, neither man survived, so no one knows for sure. Two years ago, Mallory's frozen body was discovered less than a thousand feet from the top, on the northeast ridge, perfectly preserved in the thin, cold air. But whether he'd been on his way up or down when he died, who can say?

Since first being reconnoitred for climbing in 1921, Everest has been surmounted by some 800 people. The cost has been high—the lives of nearly a hundred climbers and sherpas. Some have fallen, some have frozen, some have been swept to their deaths by avalanche. No tally has been kept of the number of toes and fingers lost to frostbite, or the cases of pulmonary oedema, but they must be in the thousands. Until very recently, few climbers had made it to the summit without bottled oxygen. Of those who tried and lived, many became extremely ill.

And so, as you can see, a climb up Mount Everest is no walk in the park. This Goddess Mother of the World is not in the habit of surrendering gracefully or without a fight. She has about as much desire to be humbled as a bucking bronco. Even without her fierce winds, bitter cold and lack of oxygen, there is the sheer magnitude of her steep, icy flanks. Which is no doubt why the Tibetans and Nepalese who inhabit her foothills, and the foreigners who come to climb, hold her in such high regard.

In early 1999, members of the International Cat Federation were advised over the Internet of the proposed feline assault on this most prestigious of mountains. As expedition sponsors, the Cat Mountaineering Society asked that local chapters submit the names of their most distinguished climbers. From this list, a hundred finalists of proven record on high peaks would be invited to Katmandu in the spring of 2000, before the monsoon. Leader of the challenge and conqueror of many tall peaks (Annapurna, Kanchenjunga, Nanga Parbat, Nanda Devi, K2), the renowned seal point Himalayan, Dawa Norquay, son of a blue Persian and cream Siamese, let it be known that he needed not only cats with high altitude experience, but those who were good at lower levels too, especially on ice. In other words, cats with suitable claws. From the list of qualified applicants, he would select hunters, porters and sprinters, all of whom would have specific functions. The hunters would supply mice and voles during the march-in through the foothills. The porters, obviously, would carry. While the sprinters, as the name implies, would make a dash for the summit from Camp 4, high on Everest's South Col. As leader, Dawa Norquay stressed that no matter what happened, it would be a team effort, with no scapegoats, no heroes. What he was looking for, he said, was a group of serious cats in top physical condition, known for their stamina and perseverance, who could work together toward a common goal. Successful candidates would have their expenses paid to Katmandu, would receive an issue of mittens and earmuffs, and would enjoy an audience with the enclave of monastic cats at Thyangboche Monastery. Here they would request an ecclesiastical blessing, as is customary with all Everest expeditions, and in exchange for a donation, would receive the traditional silk scarves to wear on the mountain.

At the end of April they began to assemble at Katmandu, arriving by air from all over the world in cat carriers stencilled "INT FED CATS MOUNT SOC EVRST EXPD." There were Abyssinians, Angoras, Persians, Maltese, Siamese, Burmese, Egyptian, Russian, Manx, Turkish, Himalayan, Tortie-Tabby, Maine Coon, Rex and Ragdoll. They congregated in an old warehouse on the outskirts of town and got acquainted. The host enclave of Nepalese cats threw a banquet at which Dawa Norquay welcomed them, gave out expedition flags and delivered a motivational speech. Then they dined sumptuously on field mice and a local delicacy, fresh caught bushtits.

It must have been quite a sight, the day of their departure for Thyangboche—a hundred assorted mountaineer and sherpa cats heading off into the foothills, single file, tails waving.

They had many advantages over previous expeditions. For example, they were able to travel light. They didn't need tents, even at high altitude, because with their sharp claws they'd be able to dig snow caves, and with their natural fur coats, they'd be toasty warm. Also because of their claws, they wouldn't need ice axes or crampons. Since this was a non-photographic trek (if, afterward, anyone doubted their accomplishment, their paw prints in the snow would be ample proof of success), they weren't burdened down with cameras, tripods and video equipment. Because of their leaping and scrambling ability, they didn't require ladders for bridging crevasses or ropes and pitons for ascending steep pitches. Because they were good at taking short, shallow breaths, they had no need for bulky oxygen cylinders, with which the slopes of Everest and other Himalayan mountains are now so disgustingly littered. And because they were so light and nimble on their feet, there was negligible risk from avalanche, that scourge of high altitudes.

But perhaps their greatest advantage over all previous expeditions was their innate ability to see in the dark. Where previous climbers had been forced to bivouac at night and, in the interest of safety, proceed only during daylight, the International Cat Federation team could take advantage of those calm, starlit hours between dusk and dawn.

After three days of trekking they arrived at Namche Bazaar, which was aflutter with prayer wheels, and the next afternoon reached Thyangboche Monastery, which is perched at 12,000 feet above sea level and overlooks the stupendous gorge of the Imja River. Here, since the weather was misty and rainy, they stayed the better part of a week as guests of the resident monastery cats. Because felines of all sorts, not just Himalayans, are revered by Buddhist monks and treated very well, Dawa Norquay and his mountaineers enjoyed themselves. They slept late, dined well and often, listened to chants and gong-playing. The chief lama, a baldheaded man in orange robes, said he'd never seen so many cats

gathered in one place. He handed out silk scarves for good luck, placed the International Cat Federation flag in his collection, and called for a huge bowl of buzz-producing *chang* (rice beer sweetened with fermented goats' milk), around which the cats crouched and lapped enthusiastically.

From Thyangboche they marched on up to the edge of the Rongbuk Glacier, where they established Base Camp at 20,000 feet. Here, half the cats would remain. They would act as support, if needed, and would lay in a supply of mice and other edibles, because when the summit team came back down, they'd be cold, tired and hungry.

Next day, fifty cats ventured out onto the Khumbu Ice Fall, that fractured, frozen river that descends from the Western Cwm. Halfway up, at 22,000 feet, they established Camp I, where twenty-five cats would remain. Next day, between the flanks of the twin peaks, Nuptse and Lohtse, the remaining twenty-five cats set up Camp II at 24,000 feet. From there, twelve climbers went up to Camp III on the South Col, at 26,000 feet. Next day, six climbers carved Camp IV out of the snow at 28,000 feet. And finally, on the calm, cold, moonlit night of May 16th, the summit team, consisting of Norquay, Thondup and Morris (two Himalayans and a Scottish Fold), dashed to the summit.

They said the view from earth's highest pinnacle was awesome. They said it was like being on the ice cap of Mars. Mountaintops stretched away in every direction, bathed in pure moonlight, like glistening sharks' teeth. Though they hadn't thought to bring banners with them, all three cats sprayed a tattered old pennant on a pole left there by a Japanese women's expedition the previous fall. It was Dawa Norquay's contention that if anyone doubted they'd actually stood atop the Goddess Mother of the World, the Japanese women's pennant could damn well be tested for DNA.

As rapid as their ascent had been, their descent was even faster. I imagine there was a good deal of slipping and sliding, because, as everyone knows, cats have less traction coming down than going up. As each camp was reached and their numbers doubled, there was general celebration. And when, two days later, they reached Base Camp, a large feast of high altitude voles was enjoyed, garnished with ice worms and newly hatched gadflies. It was a beautiful sunny afternoon, and everyone lazed about, recapitulating the achievement and their personal contribution to it.

They stayed overnight at Thyangboche Monastery, sipped more *chang*, ate leftover dumplings, and for dessert were given yak-butter tea and *tsampa*—a concoction of nuts, grains and fermented honey. Leaving Thyangboche, Dawa Norquay made mention of the fact that of the hundred cats who had arrived there the day before, fewer than sixty were now leaving. The others, it seems, knowing a good thing when they saw it, had decided to become monastery cats. "What am I supposed to tell their relatives when we reach Katmandu?" Dawa Norquay was heard to ask. "All those cat carriers to send back empty. All those plane tickets to cash in. I hope the foreign press doesn't get hold of this. They'll think we set a record for mountaineering disasters."

And that, unofficially, is a report on the International Cat Federation's millennium expedition to Mount Everest. Despite the mass defection at Thyangboche, it was, by all accounts, a smashing success. I've learned from reliable sources that a complete chronicle of the mission is to appear in the December issue of *Cat & Kitten Magazine*. Whether this is true or not, I don't know. If it is, I hope I haven't stolen their thunder.

Epilogue

The Ghost Cat

A bout a month after my friend Rolly's cat died, he saw her looking in his living room window. The cat's name was Spider, and just for a moment, he saw her familiar face. He says it gave him quite a start. I can well imagine. He says at first he feared his mind was playing tricks on him. He'd been thinking about Spider, remembering her, missing her, and figured maybe his brain had projected a mental image of her onto the window. An illusory manifestation of a subconscious vision. He had to admit, the face in the window wasn't all that distinct. But it was definitely Spider. He had no trouble recognizing her, even though he doubted what he was seeing. It must have been an emotional moment. He says he remembers wondering how the cat could be looking in the window when the sill was a good eight feet off the ground and Spider had never been much of a jumper. Not only that, there was no exterior ledge on which a cat could perch.

Rolly says he turned around and looked behind him,

wondering if what he'd seen was some sort of reflection. The trouble was, there was nothing to reflect—no photograph, no painting, no stuffed cushion in the shape of a cat. What he saw, with both eyes wide open, was a fuzzy outline of Spider's face looking in at him from outdoors. He says he was afraid to move, in case she disappeared.

And so what did my dismayed friend Rolly, a no-nonsense guy, do? He reached for his Pentax camera, which was on the bookshelf beside him. Without taking time to focus, he pointed it at the face in the window and shot the last frame on that roll of film. There was no flash, and so he wasn't sure he'd got it. The sad thing was that when he lowered the camera, which was now busily rewinding itself, he realized that Spider, if that's who it was, had vanished. All he could see out the window was my house across the street. He says he was going to phone me, but didn't, because he knew I wouldn't believe him.

A few days later, however, when he got his prints back from Primary Color Lab on Cumberland Street, he not only phoned me, he came running over. "I know you'll have trouble accepting this," he said, "and I don't begin to understand it myself, but if you want a truly bizarre anecdote for your cat book, I've got one."

Against which, after I'd seen the above photo, I found it difficult to argue. And so I beg your indulgence, gentle reader. You at least can be objective. Even skeptical. I can only say that in all the years Rolly and I have been friends, I've never known him to stretch the truth or try to put things over on people. I can't for the life of me imagine why he'd start now.